W H O E V E R
F I N D S T H I S :
I L O V E Y O U

Fr Gail

With love and

Best wishes!

Faye Moskowitz

Whoever Finds This:
I Love You

Faye Moskowitz

David R. Godine, Publisher

BOSTON

First published in 1988 by

David R. Godine, Publisher, Inc.
Horticultural Hall
300 Massachusetts Avenue
Boston, Massachusetts 02115

Some of the stories in this book were originally published as follows: "Every Airborne Particle" in *Response* and *Frontiers*; "Whoever Finds This: I Love You" as "A Leak in the Heart" in *Phoebe* and *Feminist Studies*; "The Change" in *Calyx*. All reprinted by permission.

Library of Congress Cataloging in Publication Data

Moskowitz, Faye.
Whoever finds this: I love you.

I. Title.
PS3563.088446W4   1988   813'.54   87–46372
ISBN 0–87923–746–5

FIRST EDITION
Printed in the United States of America

With love, this book is for my children,
Shoshana, Peter, Frank, Seth,
Julie, Elizabeth, and Jeffrey,
but mostly and always
for Jack

Contents

Spring comes softly to Michigan; winter is more outspoken. The wind cuts through stale gray snow to warm the earth below. Overnight, a few tender snowdrops appear in dark wet places where the snow has melted. The wet places grow; ice chunks relax and fall apart. One day the pavements are dry, and little girls in sweaters come out to chalk hopscotch squares on the sidewalks.

WHOEVER
FINDS THIS:
I LOVE YOU

Whoever Finds This: I Love You

A LEAK IN THE HEART, the doctors called it. Shifra, her own heart throbbing like a thumb caught in a door, carried the baby Chaya home and propped her in a high chair. Day after day she stuffed her with graham crackers swimming in milk, or pablum, or pieces of zwieback sprinkled with sugar and softened in boiling water. Perched on a high stool in front of the baby, she tasted each spoonful and blew on it to make certain it was not too hot. She opened her mouth wide in empathy every time the baby swallowed, but the food brimmed up, welled over and seeped out of the corners of Chaya's mouth. The food leaked out faster than Shifra could spoon it in, and one afternoon, just before the Sabbath, the baby died.

An old woman Shifra had never seen before washed

the baby and bound her jaws with a bit of flannel. After a while, the director of the burial society took the bundle away. Shifra's mother came and so did brothers and sisters with their wives and husbands and they hid the baby clothes and took down the crib and put away the high chair, but in the kitchen, Shifra found a small bowl with a flake of dried cereal stuck to its side, and she said, "David, I can't look at this place. Get me out. I'll never come back here again."

There was a way for a woman in her situation to behave; Shifra conducted herself properly, she thought. She merely did what she had seen other women before her do. On Sunday she fainted repeatedly in the airless chapel, and twice at the graveside a brother had to restrain her from throwing herself into the raw, red clay slit. Back home at her mother's house, she observed the Seven Days sitting on a low mourner's bench staring at her stockinged feet, her young face yellowed and crazed like old ironstone.

Shifra and David exchanged few words during the mourning period. When she remembered to look at him, his eyes were as shrouded as the mirrors of the house, that were everywhere draped with sheets. Even at night the two were not together. She shared a room with her mother and a sister to make space for other relatives in the crowded flat, while he slept on a cot in the living room.

One morning, finding her dressing alone, he curled his fingers around her hair, still in a thick braid for the night, and this time she averted her eyes, blushing to think she and David had ever been close enough to do the things necessary to make a baby. She could swear he had that look of wanting about him then, there in that house of mourning. It seemed to her she must be perfectly still, her arms stiffly at her sides, touching nothing, feeling nothing, loving nothing. In December, not long after the official days of mourning were over, she convinced David to take her away from Detroit to a small town some sixty miles from their family and friends.

Shifra spent most of that winter inside the house. Early each morning David left for the junkyard where he had found work with a Jewish proprietor who did not force him to work on the Sabbath. She cleaned house endlessly, polishing floors that already glistened and washing clothes that were scarcely soiled. The bungalow was small, and sometimes she woke up with little to do. Then she paced herself carefully using an intricate system of tasks and rewards she had invented for herself: wash this wall, and you may sit down for a glass of tea; iron this shirt and you may look out at the snow. Cleaning was good; she was certain of that. She was not certain of much else. If only she could discover what it was she had done to offend God so, perhaps she could make some sense out of what He had done to her.

Endless inner conversations, like dozens of crossed telephone lines, clacked in her head: Memory keeps things alive, but I know David is letting go of Chaya . . . animals are like that . . . existing as if there is no past. Everything is present for them . . . no memory except for where the food is . . . and the warmth . . . forgetting their young as soon as they are taken from them . . . But he called her his diamond . . . the star in his crown . . . and oh, how I polished her, my sweetness. She shone as though she had been dipped in pure, fresh oil . . . now she lies in the dirt . . . everything is dirty. When I was carrying her, David told me, showed me things we could do . . . when we couldn't be man and wife. He said it was allowed . . . He said, I am only human after all. I have my needs. I asked him then, what kind of women do these things? . . . He said, Shifrele, I beg you, and I did what he asked . . . Was that the sin? . . . God, help me find the dirty spot, and I will bleach it and wash it until everything smells sweet and clean again . . .

One night toward the end of winter, Shifra and David lay under their featherbed talking for a few moments before going to sleep. As she had done for months now, Shifra pillowed her head in the crook of one elbow and held on to the side of the bed with her other hand so she would not sink into the sag of the mattress and touch David's body with her own. Slowly the coal fire in the basement burned itself out, and the timbers of the little house creaked and expanded with the increasing cold. Out of habit, the two still spoke in whispers as if in fear of waking a sleeping child nearby.

David told of the salesman who came to the shop and sold Mr. Arnhoff a set of books containing all the knowledge of the world. He described the gold-stamped red bindings that looked like expensive leather and the hundreds of colored maps and illustrations. Longingly he spoke of the shiny metal globe Arnhoff would receive when he made the final payment.

Shifra could scarcely stifle a groan of impatience. Of what use to her were shiny globes? The world seemed shrunken for her like a woolen dress washed in boiling water by mistake, a dress whose shoulders refused her bowed back, into whose pockets she could no longer plunge her balled-up fists.

Still, she wanted to be a good wife and wished she had something to tell him in return; she gave him so little these days. Her mother wrote Yiddish very well. Sometimes Shifra received a letter from her, the characters crowded onto the page with a blunt nib, the vowels liberally peppered beneath each word. She always saved the letters until after supper so she would have a contribution when David told his stories. Otherwise she had little to say to him. Nothing ever really happened to her anymore, and for that, secretly, she was grateful.

Today, of course, there had been the visit in the afternoon, but she was too ashamed to tell him about it. A young neighbor, carrying a plate of cookies, had called on her, but when she answered the door, already anxious, suspicious, all her English had drained out as though her brain were a colander. She had stood in the open doorway, babbling, earlobes burning, "The same to you; the same to you."

Finally, she had taken the plate and almost closed the door in the woman's face. A hundred times later that day, she imagined another scene in which she and the pretty blonde neighbor drank tea from china cups with their little fingers delicately crooked. They spoke of many things, and her English was, of course, perfect. Instead, she had stood for half an hour behind the door, heart pounding, balancing the plate. Later she dumped the cakes in the garbage and gingerly washed the dish in the basement tubs. Goyim cooked everything with lard. God alone knew how she would get the plate back, or for that matter, whether she was to return it at all. Who could understand the customs here?

David's voice droned on. She tried to follow his words, but he confused her, speaking the names of strangers, and she resented the excitement that seemed to creep more and more frequently into his stories. She took it as one more sign that he was diluting the strength and purity of their grief. Scornfully, she mocked his clumsy English. "I'm free, white and twenty-one," he kept telling her. What did that mean? Soon he would be speaking nothing but English, and she would be more alone than ever. So she only pretended to listen for she did not really want to hear about his life outside. The child had been like a strap that bound them close. Now, unbuckled, they had to struggle to keep together.

Shifra counted the faded roses blooming along the walls, their bisected petals and leaves lovingly rejoined by some unknown paperhanger. Through the open door into the bathroom, she could see the long pull-chain to an overhead light floating back and forth in the warm blast of the floor register.

Chaya had favored a certain toy—tiny wooden chickens attached to a platform with a red ball hanging down. Shifra dreams now about that toy. She is a gaudy yellow chicken. Someone pulls the string. Up and down goes her head—pecking, picking at painted bits of corn. But her mouth is painted and she cannot open it and the corn is painted and she cannot eat it. Another jerk of the string; her painted beak goes up and down, up and down.

Now her eyelids were pulled down as though lead weights were attached to each lash. Moist, drowsy, floating, she imagined she felt the child, an infant again, nuzzling her breast. Far down inside, her womb contracted, and easily she unfolded, muscle by muscle, like a cat.

"Oh, that's good," she murmured, "so good."

Suddenly she wrenched herself awake and whispered hoarsely, "Devil, let me be!"

She pulled the sleeves of her nightdress back up over her shoulders and turned to glare at her husband. "What are you trying to do to me? Are you crazy?"

"Shifra," he said, "You are *making* me crazy."

"What if I get pregnant again? What if this child, God forbid, is sick too?"

9

"Don't worry. I promise you I'll be careful. I'll stop in time. Trust me. Everything will be all right."

"All right! That's what you always say. That's what you said before, remember? Everything is all right as long as it's what you want." Her whisper rasped on, rough as a cat's tongue. "So tell me, then, what else do I need now? I'm listening to you. Go ahead. Tell me that I need another baby for the evil eye to fall on."

David turned away from her and drew the quilt over his head. "Ai," he said into the pillow, "you don't know what you are saying."

"No, *Chachem*, only *you* know what you are saying." She sat up. "It's too soon; I'm the stupid one, but I know it's not right."

Another time, David might have tried to stop her. This time he did not move when she crawled out of the warm bed and struggled into a faded pink chenille robe. He did not call her back as she hoped he might, though she waited for a moment on the landing before she felt her way down the cracked rubber treads to the front room.

Shifra fumbled for the switch, and the plaster clipper ship on the mantel glowed in a sickly artificial sunset. A red bulb, shining from between the sails, turned the green frieze sofa a mud-brown. Even the white doilies, stiffened in sugar-water and pinned to the chair arms, looked tired and dirty in the cruel light. Cheeks burning, warmed by her anger, Shifra fell asleep sitting straight up in a slippery leather chair. Outside it was too cold to snow, but on the windows near her, frost crocheted a delicate pattern of lace.

In Shifra's dream the blonde neighbor wears an orange dress and carries an infant whose heavy head bobbles against her breast. The baby's red cheeks and round blue eyes seem pasted on to its face like little circles of color. On one side of the infant's neck a grotesque swelling hangs like a misplaced goiter. A string of mismatched yellow seed pearls, crooked as milk teeth, winds around its neck, almost hidden by flaps of flesh. Shifra can see something below the child's swollen belly that resembles the neck and spout of a watering can, but she is not sure what it is.

The blonde woman asks Shifra anxiously, "Do you think there is anything the matter with my little girl's hands?" The baby's fingers are as long as its arms and webbed between. Shifra flounders for words. She feels almost guilty because her own child is so perfect. She forces herself to touch the sick baby. "I'm sure your mama and papa have had you to the doctor," she croons.

The father (who is somehow David), answers cheerfully, "Don't worry, everything will be alright. I'm a doctor, and I've checked the baby, and its little bowels were perfectly clean . . ."

Shifra has a vision of that strange baby hanging upside down on a hook like a naked chicken in a butcher shop.

Above the window opposite her, a heavy icicle cracks loose from the eaves and shatters into brittle shards on the frozen ground. Shifra pulls the robe more tightly around her and dreams it is Succoth, the Feast of Booths, and she is a child at home in the shtetl Gorodok. Her father enters the house carrying a small wooden box. "Shifrele," he says. "Come, see what is here."

She watches as he reverently pries open the top of the box with his pocketknife.

"*Tochterle*, this has traveled all the way from the Holy Land." He lifts the lid and pulls away the grayish cotton wool that surrounds the yellow citron. Shifra can hardly breathe. The citron is perfect, without a blemish.

"Papa, I would like to be shut up in such a box, wrapped in cotton wool. Then I could stay the same forever."

Her father frowns, "What you are saying is a sin. You don't know what you are saying."

"What is the sin? Papa, why are you angry with me?"

Shifra's body was heavy when she awoke. Her veins felt as though they were filled with sand instead of blood. Like someone getting out of bed after a long illness, she was not sure she remembered how to walk. Raising the window shade, she could see an icicle drip drop steadily into an ever-enlarging circle in the snow.

Upstairs the featherbed was thrown back, and the

sheets were cold to her touch. David was gone. In the drafty kitchen, heavy graniteware utensils sat neatly on the wooden shelves she had covered with oilcloth to hide the chipping enamel underneath. She unlocked the back door and snatched in two bottles of milk, their paper caps perched crazily on stalks of ice. He must have left even before the milkman came. God knows where he went. With a sharp knife, she sliced off the frozen cream at the neck of each bottle and dropped it into a pitcher. David always took cream in his coffee.

Two chairs, lined up as if with a ruler, were tucked under the porcelain topped table. David was gone. The percolater was still in the cupboard. He didn't even have coffee before he left. Who did she have but herself to thank for this? She had pushed him too far. He was a man, after all. Where would he go alone on a Shabbos in this town where they were as good as strangers? He never worked on Saturday before. Arnhoff let the goyim run the shop on Saturdays. Now this sin would be on her head, too.

Outside was cold and alien, inside everything familiar and in its place; but David was gone so things were not in order. She put the cream away and noticed that cold water plicked slowly from a block of ice into the drip pan under the icebox. Everything is allowed to melt but me, she thought.

Gradually, thin gray morning light had surrounded the house. Her throat felt weedy, like an old downspout grown over with ivy. "Let him hang himself," she said, clearing her throat. The sun could not penetrate the thick shades shrouding her spotless windows. Shivering, Shifra crept down into the dark cellar and threw a mouthful of coal to the furnace that ate and ate and was never sated. "There," she said, grunting with the weight of the wide, flat shovel. "You and all my other enemies: choke on it!"

A fat, black spider, underbelly marked with white spots like a domino, skittered down a filmy thread in front of her face. She swung the heavy coal shovel, catching the thread on her arm. "*Gevalt!*" she screamed, running up the stairs, tripping on the robe, brushing her arms again and again against her sides. "Get off, get off!" Feeling the furry legs in her ears, down her back and crawling up to catch in the hair between her thighs.

When she finally stopped screaming, a thin moan trickled like blood out of her nostrils and through her clenched teeth. In the front room she forced herself to sit down on the sofa, then she clicked on the radio, silent during the long weeks of mourning. A sweet tenor voice rattled the cone. "Did you ever see a dream walking? Well, I did." She thought of the strange sick baby. "Did you ever see a dream talking? Well, I did . . ."

The radio blared on, but Shifra could no longer understand the English. Her teeth chattered with cold and hysteria as a perverse wave of perspiration drove sweat down the sides of her body and between her breasts. She rocked back and forth on the sofa, unaware that she moved her body to the brassy horns of some far-away dance band.

"Ten o'clock. Bulova Watch time." Early yet. In Detroit, the women would still be sitting in the balcony of the *shul*, whispering, ignoring the *shammes* as he banged his fist on the lectern and shouted for order. Why think of that now? She didn't want to be with those women who, for envy of her grief, would tear her apart like a herring. She didn't want to be sitting with them, catching the drip from her nose with a sodden handkerchief bound round her wrist, her prayer book forever blistered by tears.

She had always hated the stench of the place, the stuffy women's section smelling of fish and garlic that wouldn't wash off the fingers and of the naphthalene that seemed to be part of the very texture of the greasy black dresses so many of them wore. She couldn't stay there and become like them, waiting for the pores of their faces to open through the years and fill up with tiny carpet tacks of dirt. Away from their example, perhaps her own skin would stay milky-white instead of gradually darkening as though in perpetual shadow.

Ah, but what difference did her youth make? Long ago, the soft, sweet, brown rot set in, and one day she would push her fingers through her own flesh and touch cold bone beneath. "Shifra," her mother had said, "look at your baby one last time," and when they

15

lifted the lid, the stink of rotting flesh so astonished her, she slammed the top down on her mother's fingers.

Shifra rocked and rocked on the davenport, her arms crisscrossed on her belly. She felt a warm wet smear between her legs. My God, this too, and she had to be grateful for it. Rivka's Flora became a woman when she was only nine years old. The American teacher brought her home from school and told Rivka, "I felt sorry for the kid. She didn't know what was going on. She just raised her hand in class and said, 'Miss Chase, I have red paint all over my chair.' "

It still happens to Shifra's mother. Disgusting. She jokes about it. Calls the rags "*shlimazl* kerchiefs." Tells her daughters, "The holidays are early this month." Well, there it is: life is nothing but blood and stink, then dried-up breasts drooping to wrinkled bellies and fingers reeking of rancid fish. My mother knows, she thought, and laughs about it so she won't cry. My sister knows. Even Rivka's Flora knows, poor baby, but she doesn't know the half of it yet . . .

Like the binding of a well-thumbed book, her thoughts once again fell open to a familiar page: Mama? Here it comes again! Where is the doctor? You said he was coming. When is he coming, Mama? But I am trying. I'm trying to lie down. See, Mama, I'm trying to lie down. Yes, I know David is here, but I don't want him to see me like this. Get him out of here. I don't like the way he looks at me. Devil! You said it would

16

be all right. What do you know of it? Go! Do something. Get the doctor, for God's sake. Take my hand, Mama. Help me. Here it comes. Oh, God in heaven, Mama, look what I've done to the bed! Is that what it's like? But it's so ugly . . . so ugly . . . so dirty. I don't want it. Here it comes, and I don't want it . . .

Shifra didn't know how long she sat there on the sofa trying to wipe the scene from her head, but at last she said to herself, I will have to do something about this. In the bathroom, which she had bleached and scoured, she began to clean herself. Knocking over a stack of snowy towels in the linen cupboard, she pulled out some small squares of bird's-eye cotton. Each month, after her period, she soaked and washed the old diapers, but still faint rusty spots remained. She leaned on the wash basin, the room whirling.

Overnight, the hard water from the tap had dripped a disgusting orange stain into the white bowl. There was no end to the dirt. If she relaxed for a moment, the filth would bury her. She shook gritty powder into the basin, fingers trembling. On the soft yellow cleanser box, a downy chick stepped out of an eggshell.

Heart fluttering like a bird in her breast, she saw the sliver of steel . . . David's razor hanging from a nail . . . remembered, so long ago, the neighbor man, the goy, coming toward her carrying the writhing chicken by its spindly yellow legs, the earth frozen to steel, squeaking under his heavy boots, coming toward her, telling her through the yellow, tobacco-stained hair around his small mouth, "This is what we do to little birds who try to run away" . . . throwing the hen on the ground in front of her, lifting its wing, spreading it, a pulsing feather fan, the knife glittering, catching the sun, slitting the tendon. All the while, the chicken screaming, rasping rhythmic screams as she, Shifra had screamed then, as she had screamed when the baby tore itself out of her body, as she had screamed one other time, as she screamed now, imagining the cold steel slicing through her bushy hair and then biting the vulnerable flesh under her armpits. *This* is what we do to little birds . . .

Shifra gripped the rim of the basin, staring down at her pale knuckles, then dropped to the floor to place her cheek against the cool porcelain of the footed tub. She lay there for many minutes, her mind white and empty. After a while she said to herself, what shall I do then? Run away? Where can I run . . . to where the black pepper grows?

She stood up stiffly, bone-sore as if she had been beaten from inside, and washed her hands, twirling the bar of Sweeheart around and around. After she had flung open the window and spread their bed, she took off the pink chenille robe and dressed herself. He would be good and hungry by now and cold probably, too. What was it his fault? Who could change the world?

Downstairs, she shrugged into a heavy coat, tied a babushka around her hair and pulled open the front

18

door. The sun, mirrored in countless melting surfaces, blinded her for a moment. Chaya was gone and with her a part of Shifra that could never be alive again. There were no words to name her emptiness, no language to translate her loss. Better to bite her tongue and trust that an understanding beyond words could grow between people who ate the same bitter bread. When Shifra could see again, she turned toward the heart of town and set off to look for David.

Fanny's
Comfort Station

"THE WAGES OF SIN IS DEATH." That was puzzling enough. Fanny decided whoever had written the little pamphlet probably made a mistake. Surely it should read, "The wages of sin *are* death." The words sounded better that way, but they still didn't make much sense to her. She knew what wages were. Her father spoke often about payday and having to give the men their wages. And she certainly knew what sin was; she had thought a lot of how most of the things you did that you couldn't tell your mother about were sins.

Even reading the words made her feel sinful. All those references to Christ gave her the creeps just like the Polish pictures of Jesus that hung in her friend Catherine's house, especially the ones that showed Him on the cross, blood drops spurting from His hands

and sides like broken strings of tiny rubies. Though
no one had exactly said so, she knew there was something wrong with the very act of her being in Catherine's crowded living room, where the salt smell of
bacon lurked in the lumpy davenport and the brocade
drapes tied back with little mirrors.

As if hanging around Catherine's house all the time
wasn't sin enough, what was she doing in the comfort
station? Her mother had been plenty specific about
her not going in there again. The public bathroom in
the tiny building, down a steep flight of damp cement
stairs, harbored not only germs but the bums who were
responsible for them. Her mother knew these bums
and their tricks. They would start by asking you for a
nickel for a cup of coffee and by the time they were
through with you, they would have extracted far more
than money. Most of them were white slavers in disguise, their mouths watering to get their hands on
young girls. When Fanny asked what her mother meant
by that, she always answered, "Don't bother me." Fanny
didn't expect answers to questions like that; she only
asked because she liked to see how quickly she could
make her mother flush down to the neck of her cotton
housedress.

The comfort station was one of Fanny's favorite
places. It sat in a little park on the fringe of downtown
at a bus stop, a small red brick building with just
enough room inside for three rows of highly varnished
benches at the back, three shorter rows at one side,

and a glass showcase topped by a wooden counter. People waited on the benches, for the bus, some of them. Fanny knew others were there for the same reason she was. Otherwise why would they sit for hours as bus after bus lumbered by and none seemed to be the one they were looking for? It was comfort they wanted and what more obvious place to get it than the very place in which they sat?

Fanny was there for comfort, too. Something was going on at home that she couldn't name. She felt it hang in the air, heavy, like the weighty stillness that pervades a house just before a summer storm. At supper sometimes she found herself chattering away . . . blah, blah, blah . . . the sound of her own voice echoing back to her, bouncing off the walls her parents seemed to have erected against one another. She was frightened by the angry way the soup sloshed around in the bowl when her mother slammed it down in front of her dad.

In some ways, Fanny felt responsible for what was taking place in her house. Perhaps she loved her father too much, and her mother knew it. Fanny loved the color of his skin, red-brown where the sun reached it, pale ivory under his shirt. She loved the picture she had of him in her mind, leaning against one side of the wide barn-door entrance to the shop, one leg crossed over the other, a cigarette cupped in fingers that smelled of old copper and pennies.

So Fanny made it her business to be polite to strangers.

It was important to her that people liked her, even if they didn't really know her. Sometimes she felt like an outline of numbers in a connect-the-dot book; she needed approval to fill in her outline and make her emerge as the figure of a person. "What a nice girl you are." That's what she wanted them to say. Bobbe Raisel told her that white spots in your fingernails meant you were untruthful; one spot for each lie. Fanny kept her fists clenched when she remembered it; it was hard to protect yourself when your fingernails stood ready to betray you.

When the old woman sat down next to her, Fanny could hear a wheeze as if she had plunked herself on a pneumatic pillow instead of a hard wooden bench. "My, My," the woman said, fanning herself with an embroidered handkerchief, "Isn't it close out today? I like to die from this heat!" She juggled parcels, hand-bags, umbrella, and gloves; finally, gathering everything in her arms, she stood, turned around, and said to Fanny, "Little girl, would you mind watching my things for a moment?"

That was the sort of thing that made Fanny feel important and wanted: to be of service to someone. And although she felt a bit insulted at the "little girl" part, she said, "Yes, Ma'am, I will." You never called Jewish women Ma'am . . . they would think you were acting stuck up . . . but everyone in Jackson was gentile anyway, so Ma'am was pretty safe. While the old woman unclasped her purse at the counter where cigarettes and candy were displayed in a glass case underneath, Fanny moved closer to the bundles and rested one hand on them. She was a person who could be trusted with responsibility; even an old lady could recognize that.

"Would you like a piece of this Clark Bar?" The woman was back, wrestling with her bundles again, trying to keep them steady on the narrow shelf her plump belly left her for a lap. This offer clearly fell into the category of accepting candy from strangers, something Fanny had been warned about so many times that now that it had finally happened, she felt she was in a dream, experiencing an event that had already occurred. "No, thank you," she said, politely but resolutely.

She had learned a hard lesson about chocolate and getting something for nothing. One day her father had picked up a truckload of scrap paper from Filbert's chocolate factory. Hidden among the empty cardboard cartons lay a cache of dozens of white boxes of chocolates in their fluted, brown paper cups: caramels, jellies, toffees, nuts, and butter creams . . . pink and pale green. That evening, after he washed up in the basement as he usually did, her father brought two boxes of chocolates into the kitchen, and she and her mother laughed and chattered away about the sweet windfall. Despite the oppressive summer heat, the air felt lightened for a change; her mother's cheeks were flushed with pleasure, and her father, holding out an

opened box, said, "Mama first; take any one you like."
He laughed at how long she wavered, unable to decide
which to choose. "There's plenty more where these
come from," he said. She finally selected a chocolate,
almost shyly, and stood holding it in her fingers before
she broke it open to see what the filling was. At the
center of the candy curled a fat white worm. Her
mother swept the box off the table, and melting chocolates scattered over the kitchen floor. They ate supper
when the mess was cleaned up. No one said very
much.

The woman carefully removed her gloves and pulled
them through a ring attached to her purse. From the
same handbag, she fished out the handkerchief with
which she had earlier fanned herself, and now she
wrapped it carefully around the paper wrapper of the
candy bar. "Eating chocolate this time of year is such
a bother," she sighed. "I always use Roman Cleanser
for my stains, but then all that bleach can tear your
goods to pieces, if you don't take care." She un-
clenched her jaws slowly as if she were prying them
open and clamped down on the top of the bar with
her teeth. "I don't have a wash machine like I once
did, and wringing by hand is hard on my arthritis.
Mr. Bennet always likes to see me with rings on my
fingers; he says I have the prettiest hands." She carefully placed the Clark Bar on top of her bundles and
splayed her fingers in fans in front of her.

Fanny could not imagine how any ring had ever

been able to slip over those knuckles, big as walnuts. She didn't know who Mr. Bennet was, either, so she just cleared her throat and waited to see what the old lady would say next. "Sometimes I'd be so worn out at night, I didn't have the strength to sit up in a chair. I'd get down and read the newspaper on my hands and knees, paper spread on the floor, and fall asleep right there. When Mr. Bennet would come home and find me, he'd wake me up and tease me and say you've gone and got the stories printed on your cheek again." Overhead, a gently whirring propeller fan ruffled the pages of newspapers on the candy stand and shook loose a strand of hair from the old woman's bun, the color of cigarette ash. A hairpin fell to the cement floor with a tiny ping.

"*Watch Tower?*" said a navy blue dress, white collar and cuffs, thrusting a pamphlet in Fanny's face. "No, thank you," Fanny replied firmly as she had learned to do many times before, "I already have my own God." Watch Tower women, she felt, were not quite in the "stranger" category, because so many of them came to her door at home. Sometimes her mother talked with them for hours, standing with her arms folded behind the screen where flies buzzed a request for entrance. Afterward her mother made excuses for wasting so much time. "You can't get rid of them," she would say of the Watch Tower people; "they stick . . . like a *shmatte* to your *tuchis.*"

One night a group of young girls in white dresses

walked through the neighborhood holding lighted candles. They were singing a love song so beautiful its sound trailed behind them like the hushed scent of lilac after a spring rain. Over and over they sang until Fanny wasn't certain she really heard the words or only an echo of them in her head as the twinkling candles moved out of sight. "He walks with me, and He talks with me, and He tells me I am His own." The song and the lights and the filmy dresses filled her with the kind of longing she had felt sometimes as a little girl when her mother would relent and let her lie at the foot of her parents' bed during the worst of the summer thunder. Fanny called that feeling "homesick," because something so palpable surely had to have a name. Later, she learned that what she heard that night of the singing was a Jesus song. Knowing *that* loveliness was closed off to her, too, was simply another price she had to pay for growing up.

"I'll be twelve on the thirty-first of July," Fanny said, although the old woman hadn't asked. "Well, isn't that nice?" the woman replied. "Have you ever been to Chicago? I lived there for forty-five years. I cried when Mr. Bennet told me we were moving to Jackson, but you never know when you work for the railroad just where you'll be tomorrow." Her false teeth clicked as she snapped off another hunk of Clark Bar. "What I really used to enjoy were caramels before I lost my teeth. It was having Charlie that did it. Between constipation and the toothache, I could hardly find a place for myself so I had the teeth pulled. 'If thine eye offend thee, pluck it out . . .' " She giggled to herself, dropped her umbrella, picked it up, and went on eating.

The clock's hands on the cement wall behind the candy counter came together as if in prayer. "It's twelve noon," said Fanny. "I really need to go home to see what came in the mail. I write to our boys in the service," she confided. "The *Citizen Pat.* always prints the names of guys who want pen pals, and I always say it's the least I can do for the war effort. Of course, I don't tell them how old I am because they never want to answer you unless you're in your teens." She looked over at the woman. "Do you know Wayne Causie? He sent me his picture, and he wants to meet me when he comes home on leave. That's the part that scares me to death; I sort of hinted I was sixteen, and I think you can get in real trouble if you lie to a newspaper." She clenched her fists so her fingernails were hidden in her palms.

"Now would you just look at that," whispered the old woman, pointing discreetly with her candy bar. "Who does she think *she's* fooling, sitting there with her legs spread so you can see her entire business. Jezebel is what I call her. Whore of Babylon!"

"Isn't that pronounced 'war'?" Fanny asked, realizing she had never said the word out loud before. Gerry was a "war." Fanny had heard her mother call her "*nafke*" many times when she and Daddy were fighting, and Fanny knew that *"nafke"* and "war" were the same thing, although she couldn't figure out what Gerry had in common with the young woman who sat cracking her gum across from them in bright red dress and red beret. Gerry looked like a mother, not like a "war." She really didn't want to think about Gerry now because in some ways she liked her, even though she knew that was being disloyal to her mom.

As slowly as she could, she began inching herself away from the old woman who seemed to have nodded off, her candy eaten, head drooped forward, clutching her bundles. Fanny gave her a slight poke with an elbow, and the woman jumped. She made a strange sound. "Huh, huh." She turned her rheumy blue eyes toward Fanny. "I'm Mrs. Bennet," she said. "I lived in Chicago for forty-five years."

Disloyalty was something Fanny thought about a lot. Girls at school were always swearing to be your very best friend and then one day, there they would be on the playground standing with their arms linked around someone else's waist. That seemingly random coupling kept her always off balance. She could understand girls being mad at you if you were nasty to them, or if you didn't share your pancake-size Hostess pie at lunch, or if you told their cross-my-heart secrets, but she couldn't fathom a world where the consequences of acts you couldn't remember committing carried such unrelenting punishment.

This very minute she didn't have a single friend in

town. Everybody hated her, including her mother who was angry because she said Fanny was always taking her father's side. "Wait, wait," she had said this morning, "you'll find out what he is, that wonderful father of yours. Go to the shop; you'll see yourself what he does there with the *nafke*."

"Little girl," said Mrs. Bennet, "if I gave you a nickel, would you carry these bundles home for me? I'm not feeling too well this morning." Her false teeth clacked with a small lonely sound that set Fanny's own teeth on edge.

Only last year, a boy she had played with from time to time when she was younger, the grandson of the janitor at International Harvester near the shop, had drowned in the Grand River. Sometimes the old janitor had let them both climb on the tractors and their brightly colored attachments, each machine as glossy as some hard-shelled insect out of a nightmare, swollen to scarcely imaginable proportions. One day she had stood, part of a crowd on the banks of the river, while men in boats dragged the waters with great hooked poles looking for the boy. She pictured his bundle of a body caught in the swirling undertow like a mosquito floating on the water of her bath, crazily bobbing until the sucking drain pulled it out of sight. A few feet away, head bowed, the janitor stood with a bunch of keys dangling from his belt. No one approached him; the set of his hopeless shoulders marked him off from the curious onlookers and even from the men working at their grim task. For one more moment she thought of the boy, and then was washed in grief for those who would mourn *her* if she succumbed to the strange temptation she felt to stand at the edge of the concrete abutment—and just by accident topple over and be lost.

It's not morning; it's afternoon, Fanny said to herself, and she had other things to do besides walking old ladies home. Though she certainly wasn't going to spy on her father and Gerry, she needed to find out some things about loyalty. Didn't they say marriage was for better or for worse? Of course her mother could have been a more understanding wife. Fanny could see how often she complained—about money, about always being tired, about how dirty her dad's clothes got at the shop. No wonder her father hid behind his newspaper, shoulders hunched as if to ward off a shower of stones.

Fanny was afraid most of the time, what with the war in her house and the war in the world that caused menacing black headlines in the *Citizen Pat.* each day. The paper was filled with numbers: numbers of casualties, numbers of local boys called up, numbers of aircraft built or downed. You never knew who to trust. "A slip of the lip may sink a ship." She had stopped thinking of her home as a refuge from the outside world. When the air raid sirens wailed and her mother pulled down the heavy "blackout" shades, she discovered she no longer believed in her parents' protection; they had lost the power to shield her from the random death that might rain from the sky, or from the private battle the two of them were conducting with weapons too subtle for her to disarm.

The lead lump in her belly, the sense of loss that she carried with her always now, had started on that Sunday in December when she walked into the dining room where her father was crouched in front of the dome-shaped Philco. "Shh," he had said, raising one palm to stop her from speaking. "The Japanese have attacked Pearl Harbor." She remembered clapping her hands with excitement and then placing them both together at her lips. "We'll beat them, won't we, Daddy?" "I hope so," he said, frowning to indicate her response was inappropriate, curling his fingers around his cigarette and inhaling deeply. "I hope so."

"Mr. Bennet will be wanting his dinner," the old woman told Fanny. "Lord knows where Charlie is. I think we left him in Chicago. We lived there for forty-five years."

What a crazy old bat, Fanny said to herself. She wondered what the other people in the comfort station thought of the two of them. Did they think she was the old lady's granddaughter? What did the girl in the skimpy red dress think? And the gray-haired woman behind the candy counter scratching herself under her arms with her thumbs? Something about her coarse red face reminded Fanny of Gerry. She might be Gerry's mother for all Fanny knew; certainly Gerry had

had a mother once. What would that mother think if she knew her daughter was a "war"? Gerry was married; Fanny had met her husband, a little bandy-legged guy who worked as a mechanic at Harvester's. Maybe he worked nearby so he could spy on his wife, too.

"Little girl," the old woman said loudly, and once again Fanny felt annoyed at being taken for a child, even if it must have been perfectly clear to everyone watching that the woman was nuts. She stared straight ahead so as not to have to look into the woman's eyes again. All she really wanted to do now was to get out of the comfort station and on her way, but she couldn't decide what that way was. It was far too early to go home, especially if she were to lie to her mother and say she had been to the shop and that she was wrong; nothing was going on between her father and Gerry.

"I don't feel so good," said the voice next to her. "I believe it's my heart again. Would you help me carry these bundles home? This heat's just got to me today."

Fanny took the packages and followed the woman out of the comfort station, slowing her steps to match the funereal progress down Michigan Avenue. Once committed to going, she admired the picture she felt the two of them presented: the doddering, needy woman; the helpful young girl. "Step on a crack, break your mother's back," said Fanny. "Step on a line, break your mother's spine."

" 'A certain Samaritan, as he journeyed, came where he was; and when he saw him he had compassion on him,' " Mrs. Bennet said. "You are a good Samaritan."

"Actually, Ma'am," Fanny said, feeling a little queasy as she did at Catherine's house, "my family is Jewish."

The woman said, "Chicago is swarming with Jews; and I ought to know—I lived there for forty-five years."

"I know," said Fanny, wishing she had a friend so she could tell her all about this nutty old lady. No one would believe her anyway.

When they opened the front door, Fanny was sure at first that the house was empty. For a moment she wondered if anyone lived there at all. Inside the dimly lit front room, curtains drawn against the early summer sun, she could barely make out the shrouded furniture; she inched forward, letting the old woman lead the way. The air smelled like stale sunshine trapped for years in a paper-lined hump-backed trunk. Somewhere a clock tick-tocked, and the floorboards, covered by a thin carpet, sighed under their feet. She had a sudden crazy feeling that they might have wandered into the wrong house by mistake, that someone would emerge from one of the rooms to shout at them, threaten to call the police.

"Where do you want me to put these packages?" she asked, in a loud voice hoping to convince anyone who might be there that the two of them had no intention of sneaking into the place.

"Why it's Charlie's girlfriend, isn't it?" the old woman said, peering at her, "and you've brought me presents.

Mr. Bennet brings me little souvenirs from every city on the line." She gave a rusty cackle. "He doesn't fool me, though. I know he just wants me to forget we have to move to Jackson, but I've told him I'll never go and leave Charlie now." She had turned with one foot on the first stair tread in the front hall and faced Fanny. " 'The Lord grant that ye may find rest, each of you in the house of her husband . . .' Well, there's no rest for me . . ."

"Whose house is this, anyway?" Fanny asked, nervously interrupting. The old woman, who seemed to have forgotten her entirely now, was pulling herself slowly up the stairs by holding tightly to the banister. At the landing, she caught her breath for a moment, then turned and with a skeleton key unlocked the door to a small, dark room.

Still holding the bundles, Fanny watched the old woman ease herself onto the narrow bed with its white-painted iron frame. "I'm so tired from sitting up these nights with Charlie. You'd think Mr. Bennet was jealous the way he carries on when his dinner isn't fixed on time. He knows how bad Charlie is, and I'm run ragged trying to care for the both of them. Mr. Bennet's like a baby himself sometimes, and I don't know who to run to first."

She looked furtively around the room and lowered her voice. "You have to give them what they want, if you'll pardon my saying so. You know the joke about railroad men: you never can keep track of where they go. Sometimes I wonder how we ever got Charlie; I was so bashful when we got married. Shut your eyes and shut the lights. That's what I said to myself each time."

When Fanny's eyes had finally adjusted to the gloom, she looked around, but there seemed not to be one inch of flat surface where she might place the bundles; so with one hand she moved some dresses and shawls from a chair seat, draped them across the spindle back of it and sat down, still clutching the packages. On the dresser with its oval mirror, she saw a vanity set of ivory-colored celluloid. Photographs in gray cardboard frames—one of a solemn-looking baby and another of a dark-haired man with a great handlebar mustache—stood surrounded by a pincushion bristling like a porcupine, a woman's brown stocking stretched on a darning egg, a blue-and-white porcelain powder box and hair receiver, flowery greeting cards standing up and lying flat, letters, postcards, and pennies. Trunks and boxes lined the room, except for the wall space taken up by the bed, a night table, the dresser, and an iron washstand—its top fitted with an enamel bowl, a chipped enamel pitcher on a shelf underneath.

"Did Charlie ever get better?" Fanny asked suddenly. The woman stared at her. "How do you know about Charlie?" she asked, suspiciously, doubling over to unlace her shoes. Grunting, she pried off one shoe with the back of her heel, and then kicked ineffectually with her stockinged foot at the other. "We had to leave him in Chicago; I told Mr. Bennet I'd never leave Charlie, but what choice did I have?" She closed her eyes for a moment, then said, "I feel thirsty, would you be so kind as to give me a glass of water?"

She pointed to a carafe next to the bed. Fanny took off the top that doubled as a glass and poured water into it. She placed it in the woman's hands, but as she let go the glass tipped, and before she could catch it, water spilled into the woman's lap and down her stockings. Frantically mopping with whatever she could find—a hand towel, a cotton petticoat—Fanny soaked up most of the water. "I'm really sorry" she said, though the woman appeared not to notice. Not knowing what else to do, she filled another glass from the carafe and handed it again to Mrs. Bennet. This time, when the glass tumbled out of the woman's hand once more, Fanny realized that something was terribly wrong. The old lady sat unmoving, although she and the bed were now sopping wet.

I've got to get out of here, Fanny said to herself. She wasn't sure that she might not be arrested. What if Mrs. Bennet died and she were accused of killing her, poisoning her, maybe, with the water. Could she prove that she wasn't trying to take advantage of a sick old woman, that she hadn't followed her home to rob her? Surely if she went back to the comfort station somebody there would remember an old woman asking help of a young girl. The candy lady who looked like she might be Gerry's mother: *she* could be her witness. . . . But wasn't that why Fanny should have gone to the shop . . . so she could bear witness that her father was innocent of her mother's accusations? She needn't think of watching them as spying at all. In fact her presence might have *kept* them from doing wrong. To look at it one way, she had failed in her responsibility to her father. Instead of being his character witness, she had demonstrated her lack of faith in him.

"Mrs. Bennet," she said to the old woman who now lay on her pillow away from the sodden bedclothes. "Does anybody else live here? I think you'd better send for a doctor. Where is your husband, anyway?"

Fanny noticed that the woman's skinny legs in their baggy stockings jerked from time to time in small spasms though the rest of her body lay strangely quiet. The legs could have belonged to Olive Oyl in the Popeye cartoons, they were so thin, all wrong for a woman as heavy as Mrs. Bennet.

"I looked for him the night Charlie was so sick. I was used to it, being by myself, but Charlie kept burning up. I was scared to death, all alone with no one to spell me, and Charlie so sick. He just kept screaming and screaming until he wore himself out. And Mr. Bennet: you know how those railroad men are. You never *can* keep track of where they go. Just like sailors, with a girl at every stop." The old woman spoke to the ceiling, hopelessly, as if she were alone in the room.

"Charlie got sicker and sicker and I knew his fever was so high he would go into convulsions if I didn't do something. I picked him up there and then and put him in a basin of water we had in the room, anything to bring that fever down, and then I just went crazy, I guess. I put him back in his basket and went out to look for Mr. Bennet. He was gone when I got back, Charlie was. Still as a little rag doll lying there and I knew the moment I walked back into the room that God had punished me for not having trusted my husband. The Bible says, 'Faith hath made thee whole,' but I was worthless bits and pieces. You see, I left Charlie all alone because his sickness was an excuse to go find out Mr. Bennet."

"Where's your husband now? When did this all happen, anyway?" Perhaps if she could just keep the woman talking, she could keep her alive until Mr. Bennet or somebody came home, then Fanny could leave, hand over the responsibility to someone else. She couldn't go look for help. What if Mrs. Bennet died while Fanny was gone, just as Charlie had done when he was alone?

This entire morning felt to Fanny like a long, coiling tunnel she had been following out forever; now it seemed she had entered a dark cave that smelled of the past, a place no one had entered for years, a place where anything that could happen had already taken place, somewhere where time had stopped, so that if she ever found her way out again, it would be as if she had never been away at all. Mrs. Bennet occupied a world that didn't exist for anyone Fanny knew. How could she explain her presence here? How had she managed to get herself entwined in the life of a person whose existence she hadn't dreamed of when she set out for the shop this morning?

"I never did find Mr. Bennet that night, you know. By the time he got in the next morning, I didn't care anymore where he had been. Nothing mattered to me but Charlie, and no matter what either of us did, we couldn't bring him back. So I didn't blame Mr. Bennet for not being there. I just didn't have much use for him after that."

The old woman reached out for one of the iron bars on the headboard behind her, and slowly she pulled herself onto her side where she lay facing Fanny. "Oh, my," she said, "I do go on. Mr. Bennet will probably be home soon, and I need to fix him some supper. He's always at me for gossiping all afternoon, but I tell him he ought to try changing places with me one day, and he'd see how much time there is for talking. Charlie runs me a good race, that's for sure."

Suddenly she closed her eyes and began singing in the thin wail of a scratchy old phonograph record, beating time softly on the bedstead. "From Jerusalem to Jericho, we're traveling today, and many are the fallen ones who lie along the way." Her voice trailed off as if she had swallowed the last words, and she lay still as an August evening, asleep or dead, Fanny didn't know which.

The room with its clutter and musty scent of memories seemed to close in on Fanny. She felt bloodless, carved in stone, unable to decide whether to go or stay. From somewhere deep inside her anger welled toward the crazy woman curled on the bed for whom time had become a trickster; toward her own sense that the world cut you loose finally to find your way without landmarks or street signs—so many turnings, so many dead ends; toward her parents who had betrayed her by their failure to shelter her from what crouched at their open door. For the first time, Fanny imagined the vastness of the world outside . . . her personal insigifance in the face of it; yet, she saw, too, that the tiny cell she occupied in her own faltering orbit replicated the greater world in a scale she could begin to understand and affect.

"Charlie?" The voice was querulous. "Lord, it's cold! Can't someone bring in some coal? . . ." Fanny dragged her chair over to the old woman's bedside. Awkwardly she tucked the lumpy quilt around Mrs. Bennet's shoulders and then piled on a coat, dresses, shawls. "Charlie?" the woman asked again.

"Yes," Fanny said, reaching for the hand that lay curled near the woman's face. "It's Charlie," she whispered, gently stroking the mottled skin, "Charlie come to sit with you while you sleep." She thought of Bobbe Raisel then and the white spots, and crossing her fingers she said, "You're right; I was real sick once, but

I'm better now. I got well, you see, and we don't ever have to move; we're going to stay right here in Chicago."

Some time later, Fanny slowly withdrew her fingers from the old woman's hand. She rose and took from the bureau a picture postcard of a young woman at the seashore with an opened parasol over her shoulder. The inscription read, "I wish you were with me at Deauville." She tucked the card in her pocket as she might have done a shell or an unusual stone, proof that the morning had indeed existed. Closing the bedroom door gently behind her, she crept down the stairs to look for help.

The Runaround

OVER TWO DECADES away from the Midwest, I still long for honest cold sometimes—embody it in the fairy-tale illustration of Jack Frost, his figure formed of a wind cloud with lips puckered to expel the withering blasts and icicles sparking from his fingertips like lightning bolts. What I'm going to tell you happened in October of 1947, on an Indian-summer day in Michigan, a day all the more dear for the killing frost we had experienced the week before. I remember looking out on the backyard and seeing a few tomatoes still hanging on in low-lying places, their stems gone soft and sad, the green fruit crying out for vinegar and salt to keep them alive a little longer.

I kept a diary faithfully that year I was sixteen, a red bound volume with 1947 stamped in gold on the cover.

All through the early years of my marriage and child-bearing, it sat on a shelf in a bookcase gathering dust and the patina of promise only time can give such a record. Even during the bewildering sixties, when my children seemed more alien to me than I must have appeared to my foreign-born parents, I probed my memory, rather than the diary, for the gleanings of what it was like to be an adolescent. When I reached my fiftieth birthday, I felt that at last, both I and the record had ripened sufficiently for me to have a go at it.

What did I expect when I reopened the book? The drama of Anne Frank, perhaps, the precocity of Françoise Sagan; on a good day, surely, the musings of an incipient Thoreau. But if I had hoped for blazing insights, answers to cosmic questions, I was disappointed. Instead, I found page after page of teen keening that would have been at home in the advice columns of the very magazines I professed to abhor. Still, the reading set straight a record for so long distorted by the willful imperfection of memory and dream . . .

A prisoner of sex, I would have called myself then if Mailer had already written his book, trussed like a turkey by my inchoate longings, capable of tossing half the night on the possible ramifications of a casual "Hi" in the school cafeteria. So when my cousin, recently discharged from the army, invited me to go for a ride in his brand new Pontiac, my already tangled emotions knotted into a cat's cradle gone awry. The single eight-

by-five-inch page my diary provided each day was sufficient for most normal purposes, but Shel's official
acknowledgment of my grown-up status was responsible for a ten page college-ruled special insert, and
that was *before* our "date."

For starters, there were a great many signals I wanted
to relay to my cousin at the earliest possible moment.
I needed to have him understand I had undergone a
significant philosophical metamorphosis since he had
seen me last. The dizzy bobby-soxer he had known
was now a Zionist and a militant champion of the
single standard. Translated, this meant that in some
way I had to get to the door of that new Pontiac and
open it myself before Shel did it for me.

What I hadn't reckoned with was that Shel, after
two long years in the Pacific, had had plenty of time
to undergo some changes, too. With pin-ups of Rita
Hayworth in a nightgown and Betty Grable in a ba-
thing suit as our surrogates, came the inevitable ideal-
ization of girls back home and the elevation of the
double standard to emblematic proportions. My cousin would be determined to show me he recognized
my newly acquired young womanhood by insisting on
the car door courtesy.

Of course there had to be another factor to roil the
waters. I wanted credit for having grown up, wanted
Shel's ratification of it. By refusing to allow him a
chivalrous act, no matter what my beliefs, I risked the
misinterpretation on his part that I didn't yet consider

myself mature enough for the car door courtesy category. No wonder I filled four frantic pages the morning before Shel was to pick me up.

And then, after all that worry, the question turned out to be moot because Bobbe was visiting my mother when Shel came, and she wanted a ride to the butcher shop. There was so much commotion getting Bobbe into the front seat with her pocketbook and shopping bags and bundles that Shel hardly noticed me getting into the back seat at all.

I had dressed carefully for the outing, trying on pants, skirts, blouses, sweaters—emptying drawers, burrowing in the closet, throwing rejected clothes on the bed, on the floor—not understanding why I was paying so much attention to the way I looked for a guy who was practically old enough to be my father, and a cousin to boot.

My best friend, Malcah, sat on my bed, Indian-fashion, chain-smoking Camels and dodging underwear, giving advice. We finally settled on a flowered broomstick skirt and a peasant blouse she lent me with an elastic neckline that could be pulled down for an off-the-shoulder look.

"That'll drive him nuts," Malcah said, even though we both knew the outfit was far too summery for the season. I threw a cardigan over my shoulders so I could get out of the house without too muck flak. "Be sure to take notes," Malcah said.

I was always worrying about my breasts in those

46

days. Maybe it was comparing myself to Malcah who had, it seemed to me, perfect little tits with lovely brown nipples, while my breasts were big and floppy with no nipples at all, at least as far as I could see—and believe me, I looked all the time. Still, for a change, I wasn't having my period, my face wasn't full of carbuncles, and I didn't feel too ugly to live; in fact, I was smugly aware that the last time Shel came home on leave, I had been flat as a pancake and pretty hopeless looking. He was in for a surprise.

The alley behind the butcher shop where we left Bobbe reeked of blood and chicken doo. Red, gray-striped, and white feathers piled up against curbs and trash cans, the aftermath of an avian Armageddon. We watched Bobbe for a moment as she marched up to a tower of slatted coops of chickens, puck, puck pucking away, their frantic pinheads darting in and out between the bars. "P.U.," I said, rolling up my window.

But Shel didn't seem to be in any hurry to drive off. "Did you ever watch Bobbe blow on the chicken feathers?" he asked.

"Sure," I answered warily, "Why?"

"That's what I want to know," Shel said, looking over at me. "What's the point of all that blowing?"

I sat back, in the front seat now, a bit faint from the rich new-car smell all around me. Was this question some sort of trick, some diabolical measure of my maturity? Surely my cousin knew why old women blew on chicken feathers. "Come on," he insisted. "Why do they do it?"

Sometimes being grown-up was so tedious. Taking a deep breath, I said, "She-el, they blow on the chickens to find out which ones have the fattest *breasts!*" Then I opened the no-draft and directed the limpid autumn air toward my burning face.

We were a long time getting the conversation going after that. Either we'd both begin at once and then say, "Excuse me," our voices as perfectly in sync as the Andrews Sisters, or one of us would make a statement that would just lie there fizzling out like a dud firecracker. I had worried myself silly the night before wondering what I would do if we ran out of things to talk about, and now my nightmare was coming true before we'd hardly gotten started. I had gone so far as to actually rehearse a few gambits in case of the worst, but I hadn't mentioned it to Malcah. She would have considered that so Central High and so bourgeois.

The teen magazines I read standing up at Zukin's because I wouldn't be caught dead buying such Capitalist propaganda, were always telling you to ask your date questions about himself. I was just about desperate enough to say something unbelievably immature like, "So how was the war?" when I remembered the Marshall Plan and Taft-Hartley, but for the life of me, I couldn't figure out a smooth way to work them into the normal chit-chat. Instead, I reached over and fiddled with the radio dials. It was slowly dawning on me that I was thinking about my cousin as if he were a boyfriend, and that made me feel dishonest, like some sort of cheat. It's just that I hadn't had all that much experience with boys, and I was anxious for a chance to practice. When Shel and I did manage to say something half-way coherent, the talk would veer off suddenly like a needle jumping to the edge of a record—still I felt something happening between us, and it wasn't just my imagination working overtime, either. He would make these "courtesy" turns so that whenever we went around a corner I was thrown against him, and finally I was in on the joke too, and we were laughing so much I forgot to worry about what to say.

Earlier that summer, I had picked up a guy at the Dexter Theater. Not that I was so hard up I had to go around with men I met at the movies, but he told me he played for the Boston Red Sox, and it just happened that I had been a red-hot baseball fan when I was a kid, which is not unusual if you live in Detroit. We used to meet on one of the playing fields at Central, because you can't take a person you've picked up home to your mother, at least you can't in my family if he isn't Jewish. Besides, I can imagine what they'd say about a baseball player. Leonard Bernstein was more what they had in mind.

I kept having this fantasy that the ball player would walk over to one of the fields where someone was always playing scrub ball and that he'd grab a bat from some bug-eyed kid and knock one out of the lot the way Hank Greenberg did one legendary year at the Jewish Center, but he never did. He just wanted to sit on the grass and neck.

One day we were going at it, French kissing like mad and his hands all over me. He kept saying, "I'm Eyetalian; I've got Roman hands and Roman fingers." Before long, it was getting on my nerves. I was after him to tell me about the Boston Red Sox, mostly as a diversionary tactic, because I was really starting to question my ability to deal with older men. It didn't take a lot of brains to see he was closer to thirty than the twenty-two he assured me he was.

I had some pretty definite limits set out in those days; a girl could lose her "reputation" in an evening with the grapevine at Central as effective as banner headlines. Kissing was okay, and touching was too, but nothing above the knee or below what my blouse covered. Malcah told me men go crazy if you let them go too far, and then you were obligated to do something or it was awful for them. I didn't know what that something was and certainly couldn't ask her. There is some ignorance you can't admit, even to your best friend.

I envied Malcah's sophistication. She had already read *War and Peace* (or at least most of it), and Karl Marx, and she had been to New York alone to visit her aunt. Malcah knew all about New York cab drivers who would give you the runaround if you looked like a tourist. How do you make yourself look like you know where you're going when you don't? The whole idea drove me nuts, like something I read about dogs being able to sense your fear and how if you kept the fear smell from coming out of your pores, they wouldn't bite you. I'm not sure if I'll ever be able to go to New York because every cab driver in Manhattan will be waiting for me.

So there we were on the field with me getting grass stains all over my skirt, worrying about somebody seeing us and whether the ball player was about to go crazy; he kept trying to get one knee between my thighs while I squeezed them shut for dear life, and finally I said, pretty cooly, though my pores were giving me away for sure, "I've got to go home. At our house we eat dinner early on Friday nights."

"Aw, you're just scared," the ball player said, starting the wedging maneuver again. "There's nothing to be ascared of, honest." Then he leaned back and lit a cigarette and narrowed his eyes the way he'd probably seen Robert Mitchum do in the movies, and he said in this husky voice with smoke trailing out of his nostrils, "When I do it, Baby, they just lays back and sighs!"

That did it. Now I was certain he had reached the crazed point of no return. I stood up, not an easy thing to do gracefully, getting up off the ground without looking like a hippopatamus, and I said, "Listen, you, I've checked every roster I could find, and I don't believe you've ever been *on* the Boston Red Sox." With that I turned around and got out of there and never saw the guy again.

I don't know why I was thinking of all that while sitting next to Shel; maybe I wanted to convince myself I wasn't the naive kid I'd been the last time he saw me. At least I was savvy enough to know that even Michigan's comfortably familiar, flat terrain held pitfalls for the sexually unwary. I was almost a woman now and had had my experience with older men, but I still wasn't confident I could handle their inexorable needs.

As we drove, the city gradually petered out the way voices do in a crowd when they reach the high notes of "The Star Spangled Banner." Thickly clustered houses and stores gave way to stretches of telephone poles, and here and there, a real estate office or a gas station. We pulled up in a little wooded area, quite isolated, where fall leaves had been ground to a rich mulch on the unpaved road. Overhead, a few leaves still stubbornly blazing, made me nostalgic for the turkeys with tails spread and Indian war bonnets we used to cut out of colored paper in grade school this time of year.

We got out of the car without trying to say anything for a change. I knew something was going to happen, and I was vaguely curious about it. In a strange way, it was as if it had already happened and was simply waiting for us to catch up to it. I felt at once responsible, yet without control over the outcome. We walked for a long time, just kicking leaves and dodging the nuts that pelted us with every wind stir.

Then Shel stopped in a little clearing and began gathering great armloads of leaves, piling them on the ground where sunlight filtered through the bare branches of an oak tree. I grabbed leaves and piled, too, throwing some at him, catching bits in my hair and on my sweater, suddenly chilly, trying to warm up.

When we had a pile, bonfire-size, my cousin took off his jacket and spread it over the top. Chilly or not, this was my chance to shed the cardigan; I draped it on his jacket. We sat down gingerly because the leaves mashed to nothing beneath us. That's the wonder of autumn leaves: they fill your outstretched arms with volume but no discernible weight. Shel made a *v* of his long legs and I sat in between them as he beckoned me to do with my back snuggled into him.

It was easier talking when we couldn't see each other's faces. Shel told me about the war in the Pacific and the jungles and the mosquitoes and the heat. He told me how frightened he had been and how he used to worry he'd end up like those British war poets who never made it through World War One. This sounds silly, but while I was listening I kept thinking of Frank Sinatra and of when I was a kid, swooning over his records, loving how frail he was with that little curl on his forehead and the answering curl in his voice. It seemed such an irony; all those men bravely fighting for us and all of them, like Frank, vulnerable and frightened, needing us women to hold them.

Meanwhile, Shel was slowly pulling the elastic neck of my blouse down over my shoulders and fumbling with the hooks on my bra. I could feel him getting hard against my back, and I thought, oh, God, here we go again. He's starting to go crazy, just like they all do, and it's my fault.

I felt terrible about the war, but mostly I was sick with embarrassment. I wanted to warn him about the nipples before he got too hopeful. What would he think of me when he found I was a freak and had none? What a fraud I was. His fingers poked and kneaded inside the French bra I had blown a week's allowance on at Elite Corsetière. Still I sat looking straight ahead, pretending all this was happening to someone else, thinking of what I would tell Malcah, taking mental notes, trying to capture how it felt.

Wriggling my hips, I scooted away from him a few inches. I wasn't all that sure about this growing up business. Where could I learn the self-control the world demanded of me? Could I really will my sweat glands closed in the face of terror? Could I compose my features into the proper mask no matter what ambiguity raged beneath? All this while the meter clicked on, finally beyond my capacity to pay? In short, would I ever learn to avoid the horrors of the runaround?

By this time, Shel had at last solved the hook-and-eye puzzle. The pulled-down peasant blouse and the hiked-up bra bound me like a strait jacket. Miserable,

I crossed my arms over my chest, shivering. After a while, Shel said, "They're beautiful," and I said sadly, "But I have no nipples." He didn't laugh or turn away in disgust. Instead, he moved around so I could see his face. "But you will have them," he said. "You will."

He plucked a bit of leaf from my hair, brushing his shirtsleeve against my bare breast, finally arousing a shudder of pleasure. "The more you make love, the bigger your nipples will get," he said. Well, that was a new one on me. Nevertheless, I wasn't so naive I didn't consider the possibility that what he told me was some line I hadn't yet run into. Besides, if what he said was true, with all the fooling around I had been doing the previous months, my nipples ought to have been growing like Pinocchio's nose.

I had an obligation to keep him from going crazy; that I knew. After all, I had started it with the peasant blouse and my anxiety to prove how worldly I was. Running off at the mouth about how I believed in free love hadn't helped matters either. The amazing thing was I figured out what to do for him, but afterward I wiped my fingers over and over with his handkerchief, because Malcah had warned me if I ever got any of it on me, even on my clothes, I could get pregnant. So I wasn't taking any chances.

Shel and I were pretty quiet on the way back. The sky was beginning to cloud over, and as we passed, the autumn colors blurred like the spokes of a whirligig, when the wind picks up. Whatever had happened between us would always be there now, although I knew even then we'd never mention it to each other again. As for me, I had that day crossed another line I couldn't retrace. I needed to go home and tell Malcah and my diary all about it.

Irene

Arms outstretched, reaching, she drifts face downward in the blood-warm water, doing the dead man's float. There is always the risk, of course, that with her eyes closed, bobbing like a cork, she might be heading for the deep end. She prays for a miracle: Red Sea parting to reveal wave-combed furrows, the shells of men and ships. A madwoman is rocking in the blood-warm water; imprisoned breath rattles at the bars of her rib cage. In this white-tiled space, air so heavy that it would be rain outside, she floats on Demerol dreams. Miss Kelly in whites waits at poolside, whistle clutched, ready to pierce the air like a scream when the baby, expelled at last, a cork from a bottle, surfaces, and the test is passed . . .

Irene lay face down on the tumbled bed, slowly

drifting back to consciousness. She had that sick, hollow feeling she remembered from childhood mornings when the coal furnace died leaving a cold house with a grate full of dead ashes to shake down. The night before, Irene vowed for the hundredth time to fix Carl breakfast, but he was up and gone to the office long before Robbie, banging his crib against the wall, woke her. Rock-bump! Rock-bump! Her pillow couldn't smother the sound of him.

Goddamn Marie, she thought, late again or worse yet, not going to show at all. Irene kicked off the covers, pulled her nightgown straight, and walked barefoot downstairs to the kitchen. "Okay, okay, Mama's coming," she yelled, pouring cold milk into a bottle, screwing the nipple on tight.

In his room, Robbie, eyes glistening with tears, knelt on a pile of twisted bedclothes, looking out at her from behind the bars of his crib like some forlorn monkey. She stuck the bottle in his mouth and put him on the dressing table. Too wet to leave him like that with the pee leaking out of his rubber pants. "Jesus, Robbie," she said, "you've banged a hole in the plaster with all that rocking." She changed his diapers and threw them into a metal diaper pail, releasing a sharp stink of ammonia and pine deodorizer when she opened the lid.

"My God, that's awful," she said, but the baby, sucking on the bottle, didn't answer her. "Talk to you and talk to the wall, it's the same thing." She put him back in the crib on top of a clean sheet and threw in a teddy bear. After a moment, she added a Playskool cone of graduated colored rings on a wooden spindle. She worried that there was something wrong with him. Even her neighbor's baby, who was supposed to be autistic, said his own name. Robbie wouldn't say "Mama" for God's sake. She wandered around her bedroom for a few moments, picked up a pair of Carl's shorts draped on the bedpost, dropped them on the floor. Then she crawled back into bed where she slept until the rhythmic rocking woke her again at eleven-thirty . . .

When Irene met Carl, she was in her last year at Central High School. She was still getting lost sometimes in the vast building, and at night she dreamed she couldn't find her classroom or that she was late for an exam. Carl, a senior at Wayne State University, was to her eyes an older man. He was twenty-two, an army veteran going to school on the GI Bill, and she, not having much else to do, married him after they had gone together for eight months.

Irene attracted a brief flurry as the first girl in her senior class to be engaged. She took some pleasure in hugging her schoolbooks to her chest in such a way that the small diamond Carl gave her would be visible to girls who had snubbed her in the past. Irene didn't plan to go on to college. The grown-up world was crumbling. She wanted a solid foundation: marriage, a house, and family, something to dispel the sense she had that the earth was shifting like beach sand under her feet.

After their honeymoon, Irene and Carl moved into a little efficiency apartment in Detroit. Jobs weren't easy to get for women with all the men coming home from the service, so she stayed home and got jittery from cigarettes and the cups of black coffee she believed went along with marriage and maturity. She had all the time in the world, but she never did manage to return all the duplicates of wedding and shower gifts they received. For years they carried three electric coffee makers, two toasters, and a Proctor and a G.E. iron, wherever they moved.

Fuller Brush decided to take on a line of Dagget and Ramsdell cosmetics later in the year she married, and so for a few months Irene sold beauty products door-to-door in her neighborhood. Every morning she would put on pancake, rouge, lipstick, and mascara, more make-up than she was accustomed to, but it was usually afternoon before she got up enough nerve to go out on the street, feeling deceitful, as if in disguise.

The trouble was she kept running into women as moorless and lonely as she was. The hours she spent chatting in their spotless homes or apartments never resulted in any sales. One woman, whose husband had died of a heart attack, showed Irene a closet where dozens of four-in-hand ties, already knotted, hung ready to be slipped over the head and pulled tight. Her husband had been an efficiency nut, she told Irene, forever worrying about wasting time. She wasn't up to giving his clothes away yet.

If Irene did sell anything, it was always to some poor wretch who was spending the grocery money on perfume. Then she felt guilty and gave the woman dozens of samples of lipstick and cologne Irene had to buy from the company. It wasn't long before Carl showed her she was losing money by working. Soon after, she returned the sample case and stayed home.

Irene got involved with canning for a while, mostly tomatoes. She had vague ideas about international cartels and big business. Canning seemed elemental to her, a way to side step one layer of commerce that stood between her and the food she ate. Carl took her to the Eastern market on Saturdays, and they bought bushel after bushel of tomatoes. For several frantic days after that she would scald and peel and boil, always conscious that the heavy fruit was ripening and rotting before her eyes. No matter how quickly she worked, and Carl too, sometimes, the apartment reeked for days of decaying tomatoes. Once she tried canning applesauce but otherwise she stuck to tomatoes, unable to truly overcome her generation's mistrust of anything that didn't come out of a tin can.

She sent for USDA pamphlets that advised her of safe ways to preserve apples and tomatoes; still she boiled the contents of each jar for an hour before she would let Carl taste it. The canning binge lasted one fall, but she got tired of having to boil the food all the time and started buying tomatoes in cans again. Irene and Carl took the remaining home-canned food with them when they moved, along with the duplicate wedding presents. They stored the lot in the basement.

Mostly Irene slept, deep, dreamless sleep, awakening still tired, not knowing where she was, not thinking she was somewhere else, simply lost. When her mother phoned, as she did every morning, Irene heard the ring but did not answer, burrowing her head under the covers, feeling the clang in her jaw like a toothache, long after the ringing had stopped. Later she would tell her mother she had been out; "shopping," she would say vaguely. Her mother would understand that. She shopped endlessly, driving from one center to another in hectic pursuit of shoes. She had dozens of pairs, and they all hurt her feet. Irene thought her mother was crazy to buy pair after pair of spike heels when she knew she would never be able to wear them.

During the war, Irene had begun to fear most of the world would be destroyed before she ever really got a chance to see it. She remembered watching newsreels of bombs leveling entire sections of European cities whose names she knew only from books. There won't be a London by the time I'm able to go there, she told herself with a piercing sense of loss. Now the atom bomb would take care of what was left. She felt cheated, unable to believe anything was substantial— like her little brother the day she stood in line with him for hours at Hudson's so he could meet Bill Boyd.

"Is that really Hopalong Cassidy," he had said afterward, "or was it only a dream?"

She wondered what other young married women did with their time, but she didn't feel close enough to anyone to ask. Her few acquaintances, her cousins, the woman in the next apartment didn't reveal much. If they were worried about the world crumbling, she couldn't discern it from the animated way they talked, half disparagingly, half proudly about waxing and polishing "my" floor, "my" furniture. She always said, "I scrubbed 'the' sink." Perhaps that was her problem: She had no sense of proprietorship about anything, not even a toilet fixture.

"You need to get out of yourself," her mother said. Irene thought that was an interesting way to put it for she often felt her spirit leaving her body, dragging along behind her, a shadow she was forever tripping on as if it were the hem of a too-long coat.

Irene read an article in the Sunday *Detroit News* that said practical nursing was a profession much in demand. Nursing seemed a good way to get out of herself; so Irene signed up at Goldberg Trade School where she took notes in a loose-leaf binder and changed bedsheets under a life-size dummy with a peeling nose who smelled like her dolls did when she used to leave them out in the rain by mistake. The dummy was called Mr. Featherstone, and the week they practiced giving him an enema, Irene stopped going to Goldberg Trade.

Carl was finishing his last year of law school when Irene forgot to insert her diaphragm one night. After that, she didn't bother anymore. She told her neighbor about missing her period but not her mother who had been after her lately with suggestions about "starting a family." Carl didn't seem to notice anything at first, although Irene was convinced she felt nauseated a day after conception. She gave up cigarettes and coffee because they made the nausea worse and lived on soda crackers and malted milks for which she sent Carl out late at night when most of the nearby drugstores were closed.

One night she wakened him at two in the morning saying she would die if she did not have a chocolate milk shake. Carl was gone a long time looking for an all-night drugstore, and when he finally got back with the shake, she found the soda jerk had forgotten to put in any ice cream. She cried bitterly about that. Carl tried to treat the whole thing as a kind of joke. That made her so angry she didn't speak to him for two days.

After Carl graduated from law school and began studying for the bar exam, Irene's parents gave them the down payment on a tract house in Oak Park, a bald, newborn suburb outside Detroit. When Irene was in her ninth month, she and her mother picked out baby furniture to be delivered after the baby came. Irene chose "early American" to go with the other furniture they bought for the new house. She wanted the house to reflect her desire for tradition and connection.

When they were finally settled in the new house, Irene bought a Singer sewing machine on time without telling Carl. She planned to save the money for the payments by sewing most of her layette. Unfortunately, she had no car with which to get to the free sewing lessons in Detroit that came with the machine. The clothes she managed to sew, following the machine's instruction booklet, were all misshapen; the sleeves had great bumps of material under them, and she kept breaking the needle, so after a while she put the Singer in the basement along with the duplicate wedding presents and leftover jars of tomatoes.

The second time Robbie woke her, Irene decided to stop fooling herself about Marie. She really wasn't coming in to work today. She was more disappointed than she cared to admit, not only because the house, as usual, looked as if it had been ransacked, but because she looked forward to Marie's company. She was supposed to get out of the house a little on the day Marie gave her; often she found excuses to stay home, and then she followed Marie around, carrying an ashtray, smoking cigarettes, and gossiping about Marie's family and her own. Sometimes Marie had time to bake an apple pie or fry some chicken for supper. Then Irene felt especially happy. She liked to have her house smell homey, the way a house should. Irene was not naive enough to think that all black women loved the white babies they cared for, but she knew Marie loved Robbie. She never worried about leaving him with her.

Irene dialed her mother's number, clicking off the digits automatically. (She had tried dialing the number in the dark one night and found she could do it.) "Ma," she said, "Marie didn't show for a change, and I've got to go shopping. There's not a drop of food in this place." She interrupted the crackling at the other end. "No, I don't *want* you to go shopping for me; I've just got to get *out* of here." She was angry at herself for whining, but she dropped the receiver in its cradle, not waiting for a reply.

Irene cried along with the baby while she mixed his cereal and hot milk. "What's the matter?" she kept saying, not certain of whom she was asking the question. When her mother walked in an hour later, the house was presentable and Irene had her coat on. "It's murder outside; you'll die in that coat," her mother said.

Handing her the baby, Irene took the car keys from her mother who said, "I hate to say this, but you'd better tell Carl to do something with that grass." It was true. In the thin spring sunlight, the front lawn looked patchier than ever, as if it were suffering from some sort of mange. Carl bought grass seed like it was going out of style, but Irene had warned him nothing would grow on heaved-up builder's clay. More topsoil was what they needed. He paid about as much attention to what she said as the man in the moon. Grass was complicated for Carl—all tied up with maleness and the pioneer image he had of himself, battling the elements, subduing the wildness of the suburbs.

Irene maneuvered her mother's red-and-white two-toned Pontiac onto Coolidge highway and headed for Northland Shopping Mall. The pavement, an unhealthy white, reminded her of a coated tongue. She kept her eyes averted from the gray cinder-block shells of buildings going up on either side of the newly widened road. She found she lost her sense of place in the world when, each week, new buildings changed the contours of landmarks she was just getting used to.

"What'd they do, move the Ford plant out here?" she muttered, weaving in and out of lane after lane of solidly parked cars. She spotted an empty slot at last, noted the location on the back of a check stub, having spent the better part of an hour searching for her car the last time she went shopping, grabbed her purse and locked the car door. Northland's spewing fountains and glinting sculpture always disappointed Irene. The deliberate carnival air only made her clutch her purse suspiciously. She remembered the old Hudson's downtown: staid, dependable, the rush of perfumed air when you pushed through the heavy revolving door, the chocolates piled into sweet towers, the gray-haired sales ladies who would never think of saying, "That's not my department."

The new Hudson's at Northland rose only a few stories as though it intended to remain earthbound, unwilling to present too visible a target from any distance. Only a bulbous tower announced its presence to the sprouting surrounding suburbs. Irene wanted an entire city block of floors going up, up, up so that from the top floor, where mothers would be lured by their children to the toy department, shoppers swirling on the streets far below would shrink to Lilliputians. Nobody went downtown anymore. People said the city of Detroit was dying. Irene once thought Hudson's would never die.

Circling the main level, already dizzy, Irene stopped at the book department to leaf through the best-sellers. Actually she didn't have the patience to read anything but murder mysteries; those she devoured so obsessively it wasn't uncommon for her to go halfway through an Agatha Christie or an Ellery Queen before she realized it was one she had read before. In leather goods, Irene fingered a marked-down 1952 diary for many minutes before she rejected it: no bargain; too much of the year had already slipped by. She spritzed herself with Arpège from the atomizer on the perfume counter and felt the satisfying lift of something for nothing. A benign form of cheating the system, she told herself.

The glancing forms bouncing off mirrors that lined the walls confused her; once she turned the wrong way and bumped her nose against the image of a white-faced, dark-haired young woman in a winter coat too heavy for the season. She said, "Excuse me" before she saw the woman was herself. Purposeful shoppers jostled her with their purses and parcels. When she reached the book department again, she was sweating, afraid she might faint.

In the ladies' lounge, Irene sat and smoked a cigarette with her legs crossed. The sound of running water in the row of sinks and the many small explosions as the toilets flushed were not unpleasant to her. A black woman in a pink uniform went in and out of the stalls carrying a bottle of pine disinfectant. Irene knew she was different from the other women Marie worked for; that was one of the few things she was proud of. She would understand if Marie had trouble getting up some morning, so why was it that Marie would never call to say she wasn't coming in?

The pink lounge swarmed with girls and women. All of them seemed in a hurry; they checked off lists, fumbled through their parcels. Irene wondered if any of them ever got up in the morning without knowing what they would do for the rest of the day. She saw a woman, about her age, jerk a little girl by the arm, then slap her face. Another woman sat at a round stool in front of a mirror and poked at her teeth with a toothpick. She would not do any of those things in public, Irene thought.

Where was her place among all these women? "The apple doesn't fall from the tree," her mother was always telling her. "Far from the tree," Irene would say, automatically, but she knew what her mother meant, and she feared it, feared the shoe boxes with their tissue-wrapped spikes. The world felt diminished to her, its depths plumbed and found wanting. Yet the shoppers who surrounded her seemed unaware of all that had been lost. Six million vanished as if the sea had closed over them. Was she the only mourner?

Well, what could she do about any of it? She smoked another cigarette and looked at her watch: three o'clock. Time to go home. Traffic would be picking up soon, and she hated to drive when the roads were jammed. And the groceries—there was no way she could face the supermarket today. Maybe she could talk Carl into taking them to a drive-in again.

Not far from the lounge exit, the Lanz collection hung together in an alcove decorated like a Swiss chalet. Something about the way these particular clothes were made pleased her more than most things did. She admired the details: the tiny buttons covered in fabric, the batiste linings, the deep hems. She wanted closets full of them, wanted to touch them, read the labels that described each dress, the fabrics used, the care required. She could not afford their prices, of course, although her mother would buy her one of the dresses if she asked. Still, that wasn't the point. One dress wasn't what she was looking for.

Grabbing an armload of Lanz dresses on their hangers, Irene took them into a dressing room. Outside, a saleswoman leaned on a pillar, looking at her fingernails and then at her watch. The dressing room, painted antique white with plush blue carpeting, was furnished with a spindly curve-legged chair and a round platform on which to stand when a hem needed to be put up. Irene hung up the dresses, took off her heavy coat and dropped it on the platform. She tried to see the back of her head in the three-way-mirror. She always wondered if she could recognize herself from behind.

Dreamily, Irene stroked the dresses: this one a silky cotton, that one a fragile lawn. She fingered the buttons, the smooth zippers in their plackets, a yellow Peter Pan collar lying flat like two half-slices of lemon. She selected a two-piece dress of orange-and-white checks so fine they blended to milky apricot. Pulling her own dress over her head, she dropped it on her coat and stepped into the orange skirt. The dressing room was warm, but the bare skin of her arms prickled with cool excitement.

Outside the heavy curtain, a bored voice asked, not hopefully, "Need any help?" Irene started, her pulses banging. "No, thanks," she answered swallowing, "I'll let you know." The zipper of the orange skirt would not slide up. Too small, but if she lost a little weight . . . She put her arms in the orange-checked top, the fabric delicate as a handkerchief, and fastened several of the dozen tiny buttons filing down the front of the blouse. Then she unpinned the Lanz instructions and the Hudson's price tags and slipped them into her coat pocket. In a few seconds, she had put her own dress over the new one and was buttoning her winter coat.

"Nothing worked," Irene said to the saleswoman who was still leaning against the pillar. "Sorry." Irene's blood sang in her ears. For the moment she felt exhilarated and invulnerable. Deliberately, she slowed her pace, even stopped at the hosiery counter to debate the relative merits of "warm beige" and "suntan" with a clerk who wore her glasses on a long gold chain.

When Irene parked at the curb in front of her house, she saw her mother sitting on the front steps, watering the grass. "I hate to say this, Irene, but *you* should be doing this once in a while." She snaked the nozzle up and down a few times for emphasis. Irene was silent. She couldn't get up the path because her mother held her at bay with the hose. "And the thing I'm really worried about is why doesn't this baby talk?" She indicated the stroller with her head.

"His name is Robbie," Irene said, "and maybe he doesn't have anything to say." Her mother screwed the nozzle shut, reducing the insistent stream of water to a tender rainbow bubble, and then a small trickle that ran up her forearm. "That's you, Irene; nobody could ever tell you anything."

Irene took off the Lanz dress in the bathroom and dropped it in a clothes hamper. After her mother left, she put it with the other Lanz dresses in the basement near the wedding presents, the canned tomatoes, and the Singer sewing machine.

Every Airborne
Particle

THIS IS WHAT I'm willing to remember: the hot summer afternoon passes slowly as though it has nowhere in particular to go. In the grudging shade of a limp maple, a brown wicker carriage stands, and an infant sleeps fretfully under the white mosquito net, his eyelids twitching, the corners of his mouth turning up from time to time in an involuntary grimace that mocks the name of smile.

I guard my baby brother from the cats who will surely come, my mother says, to suck his breath away. I roll lazily on the thirsty grass, kicking the buggy with my bare feet when the baby cries. Even the bluebottles lack the energy to bite, lulled to stupidity by the businesslike heat. And I think about Nora and Jeannie and the old neighborhood. I try to remember how it was before the baby came.

73

One day when the snow was all pure and white like a new fur muff, Nora and Jeannie and I made a "fox and the geese" track, a giant ferris wheel in the snow. We ran and chased each other and sucked the little hard beads of ice from our mittens. Afterward, we took an old dead branch and drew a heart and put our initials in it, one after the other. The world was white that minute and quiet like a huge movie theater just before the show begins. We looked at each other and didn't say anything for a while and then Nora laughed and threw snow down my back, and all of a sudden we all screamed and the day cracked into a picture puzzle.

Now I slam my heel into the buggy. The baby jerks his arms up over his head and begins to wail. Looking toward the house, I stand up and rock the buggy wildly from side to side. The infant's face becomes a scarlet poppy with a black O in the center. My mother bangs the screen door and comes running from the house.

"What did you do to him?" she shouts.

"I didn't touch him."

Snatching the baby from the carriage, the mother cradles him in her arms. She comforts him with soft shushing sounds.

"Mama, I have nothing to do."

"Nothing to do! You had something to do and you didn't do it. Go away. Go find someone to play." She bends to the milky sweet-sour mouth of the infant, and her face disappears.

"There's no one to play here." I pull one lank brown pigtail across my mouth for a moustache. "Everything was better at the old house."

"So go back to the old house if it was so good over there."

A moustache and a burglar's mask now. "But, Mama, you said it's too far to go. Besides, it's not my neighborhood anymore. Why did we have to come to this place? Why can't we go back? I just want it all to be exactly like it was before."

My mother hesitates for a moment, then flicks her hand at me in a wordless gesture that says clearly, I have troubles of my own. She carries the baby inside and goes upstairs to nurse him. On a vine, next to the still-trembling screen door, pale blue morning glories have shut themselves up for the day.

I stand around for awhile with my stomach knotted like a cat's cradle. I'm hungry and want something but I know it's not eating I want. So I got into the house and holler, "Ma, Ma," and she calls down, "I'm up here with the baby." I say, "I'm going for a walk," and she says, "Stay away from the tracks," and she doesn't even come to the top of the stairs to see if I have broken a leg or something, so what do I care? It serves her right if I do go to the tracks and get my tongue frozen to a rail.

I take an apple from the icebox and four cigarettes from a pack of Luckies my father has left on the smoking stand. Before I go out the door, I turn the iceman's sign to seventy-five pounds. I don't know what you do to get noticed around here.

Once upon a time, but not very long ago, some people named Slaughter had a little girl called Eva. Her hair was plaited into two thin braids and a red line ran down the middle of her head where the part was. Mr. and Mrs. Slaughter were not Eva's real parents. They got her from an orphan home, and they kept saying they would adopt her when her trial was over; but sometimes Mrs. Slaughter said if Eva was bad, they would send her back where she came from. All the mothers said wasn't it too bad that Mrs. Slaughter couldn't have a baby of her own, but a miracle happened and she did. One day some of Eva's friends came to play with her. They knocked on the front door, but no one answered. Then Mrs. Slaughter came to the upstairs window with the baby and said that Eva didn't live there anymore. A girl who was Eva's best friend cried when she heard about it, but some boy said Eva's hair always smelled like turpentine, and who cared anyway? After awhile, some kids moved into the neighborhood who had never even heard of her.

The heat bounces off the pavement in cellophane sheets. Under my feet, the soft, sticky tar wants me to slow down, but I have to get where I'm going. Eileen's father put their old cat in a paper bag and left her out in the country, but she climbed out and found her way back without stopping. I walk up Grinnel Street past the broken-down house where the man lives with all the dirty kids and the woman my mother says is not his wife. Sometimes my mother is so dumb you can't believe it. How can he have all those kids if she isn't his wife? When I pass Markowski's grocery, I rap on the window and wave at Wanda. She has the most beautiful blonde hair even if it does come out of a bottle.

The houses begin to get smaller and farther apart. I can smell the Consumer's Power Company. I'm tired of walking, and the heat is making me forget what I'm looking for. Over and over I say, "Fudge, Fudge / tell the judge / Ma's gonna have a new ba-by." Pretty soon I'm marching to the beat of it: fudge, fudge, tramp, tramp.

Now I'm past the power plant and almost to the tracks. I can see the big sign shaped like an X that says, "RAIL/SING, CROSS/ROAD." Every time I get near those tracks, I think about the boy whose mouth froze to the rail, and I get sick, so I always start saying dumb things out loud so I won't remember it, and now I holler, "Fudge, fudge!" It just doesn't do any good. I can feel my tongue sticking to that icy rail and then, all bloody—coming off. I start to run now, along the tracks and over the ties.

Like cast-off toys, a collection of shanties is flung around the back of the coal yard. Wispy black smoke from scavenged coal feeds a few fires, and here and there, a sooty coffeepot bubbles. Outside a corrugated metal shack, an old man with a pinned-up pant leg stirs something in a rusty tin can. He doesn't look up as I pick my way impatiently through the discarded wine bottles and battered Campbell's soup cans.

Taylor's place is the grandest of all. It's made out of an old moving van that nobody wanted anymore, and he has it fixed up all neat inside like a playhouse with everything just where it belongs. But the door is shut tight, and I don't know what I'll do if Taylor isn't there. I knock and knock on the door, and water runs down my cheeks—I can't tell whether it's tears or sweat for Taylor doesn't answer. I knock again. The van door slides open a crack, and I hear Taylor's voice. "Who the hell is it?"

"It's me, Taylor. Let me in."

The door slides open a stingy bit farther.

"I thought I told you not to come here again."

Taylor knows my parents don't like me to see him. When he worked for Daddy, he was always coming to the shop sick. My father would sing *"shiker is der goy"* behind his back and pretend to drink from a bottle. It all has something to do with Taylor's being a gentile, I guess. "Let me in, Taylor," I say. "I have a present for you."

Taylor looks around. "Hurry up. Get in here then."

Inside the fetid van, breathing ceases to be automatic. One clumsy square has been cut out of a side wall with an acetylene torch, but even this opening has been shrouded by a dusty sugar sack. The flickering light of a Coleman lantern reveals an unmade cot, a wooden table and stool, and an enameled dish pan filled with mismatched crockery.

It's dark inside the van but there's a lantern to give light, and it's very cozy. Taylor has the little stove going even though it's hot outside. I don't mind it a bit. The warm and the dark always make me feel safe somehow. I give Taylor the apple and cigarettes, then I strike a match for him to smoke a Lucky. Maybe Taylor has been sick again. In the match flash I see he has sprouted a grayish stubbly beard and his eyes are red and swim in water. His mouth tastes of sour Concord Blues, and the whole place stinks like laundry piled up in the basement. Poor Taylor, I know he'll never get a wife to take care of him now that Marlene is gone.

I sit down on the cot next to Taylor and look at the calendar of the beautiful blonde lady with hair like Wanda's. The picture says, "Danger: Soft Shoulder." It doesn't make sense. I tell Taylor how I miss Nora and Jeannie and about the new baby. While he listens without saying a word, he drinks from a bottle of Arrow's Blackberry Brandy. After awhile, it's time for the candy.

Taylor says, "I have a surprise for you." He holds out a box of fat little chocolates that have a curl on top of each one. I bite off the curl . . . umm, and suck out the sweet filling, then chew up the cherry. I'm warm and drowsy and Taylor whispers in my ear, "Have I told you the story about what happened to Marlene?"

Now Taylor knows he's told me that story a hundred times. I guess it's like a game you play with rules, because it's always the same. I always eat chocolate and then Taylor tells me about the accident.

Taylor says he's tired, and he stretches out and holds me carefully around the waist. "Keep me company," he says, and I lie down next to him on his little bed. The sheets are wrinkled and soft like old magazine pages that have been read and read. He's so tall he reaches from one end of the cot to the other. I can fit neatly into the scooped-out curve his body makes when he curls up a bit. I can't see his face, but I can feel him hugging me close, keeping me from falling.

He says Marlene is not dead, only sleeping till Christ will wake her up, and she and Taylor will be together in the hereafter. I see a picture of her in my mind . . . resting on a black velvet bed with her arms folded on her chest. A transparent crystal cover arches over her.

Then we talk some more about the hereafter. Taylor says it's not scary. "Listen to the words," he says, "here . . . after." He tells me it just means that it will be the way it is here with everyone you love, not strange and different at all, but it will be *after*, do you see?

There's a certain warm sweet thing Taylor does that makes you feel all chocolate inside, and it's a good feeling, but afterward you think maybe a soda cracker would be the thing to have. If my mother knew where I was right now, she would probably be knocking the door down.

I have an idea that the here is not quite the same as now, but only like a snapshot of it. I'm afraid all the right people won't be in the right place when the picture is taken. Who arranges everybody and makes sure it's the very second you want for your hereafter? What if someone's missing or the wrong people get in? I just don't think it will work because it's never really here. The minute you think it is, it's already passed.

Taylor is holding me so tightly, I can hardly breathe, and the kerosene from the lantern is making me dizzy. Taylor tells me how he will never love anyone again but when I grow up maybe I can be his girl; he's crying, and then his voice gets all funny, and I think maybe he's going to throw up or something. After awhile he says, "You better get out of here."

The door slides open—a slow motion camera shutter—and a bright battering ram of sunshine dashes against the interior van wall. White dust motes dance a moment in the blackness that is light, and the van is dark again. Outside the light is a surprise the way it is after a Saturday matinee when you have been inside so long you think dark's the way the world is.

On the way home, I remember one night when it was too hot to sleep, and I took my pillow downstairs to lie on the living room carpet. I saw a strange light in the kitchen doorway, and I was afraid, and wanted to holler, "Fire!" but I crept closer and saw it was the *yarhzeit* candle for my grandmother, sputtering in the bottom of the glass. There was only a wick and a tiny pool of melted wax left, but the light was strong, and fire shot shadows brighter even than in the beginning.

My father came down and we sat on the front porch and listened as, far away, the thunder growled in another town. I had that same hungry feeling I have now, and I thought this whole sky is like a candle that can't bear to go out, and I'm crying because I don't know who it's lit for.

At the door, my mother stood in her nightdress. "Al," she said, "it's so late, she should be asleep," but my father drew me close and said, "It's all right, let her stay a little while."

Thelma

SOMETIMES THELMA FELT her shoulders slump forward from the sheer weight of it, plunked there in the middle of her face as though a sculptor had slapped on a blob of clay, then lost interest before the piece was finished. Whatever romantic excuses she might find to explain its existence, the nose remained: fat, hooked, and long—a nose that would have lent character to a mature man with a head half again the size of hers.

She dreamt so often the nose was gone that she was forever touching it to see if it were really still there. Well, there was no need of touching just now; the chromium fittings behind the long counter reflected her image, over and over—the body and face distorted as in the mirrors of a fun house, her nose more grotesque than ever. I'm too ugly to live, she told herself.

Slipping the dime tip into her uniform pocket, Thelma placed the empty mug on top of the other dirty dishes, threw the crumpled paper napkin in a waste bin, and mopped the counter with a rag. Ten minutes to eleven. She yawned and straightened her shoulder blades, but the burning pain persisted. Thank heaven it was almost over. You had to be nuts to work a full day and try to finish school on top of it. The sky was still turning from black to gray when she left the house this morning; she hadn't had a minute of her own in almost sixteen hours.

At breakfast, her father, unshaven, his work pants' suspenders drawn up over a dingy union suit, gulped his second cup of coffee with a little expiration of breath after each swallow that made Thelma's stomach turn. In a pink chenille robe and felt slippers, her mother padded back and forth between refrigerator and sink, packing her husband's lunch: four center slices of rye bread daubed with liverwurst, a Hostess pie (apple), and a tall thermos of coffee.

"You're not eating, " she said to Thelma, accusingly. Big joke, thought Thelma. Eat what? They were forever "out" of things; at least that was how her mother put it. And what there was, "day-old" bread from the factory outlet, tired fruit and vegetables the produce man should have thrown away, or gristly meat and bones her mother begged for the dog they didn't have, Thelma refused. She couldn't forgive her mother the lie that they were poor.

84

"In some houses they scare kids with the boogie man," Thelma once told a friend. "In our house it's the Depression." Why wouldn't her mother let go of the bad times? Carpenters made a decent living now, and her father worked Saturdays to keep up with all the jobs he had waiting. Of course they weren't rich like most of the kids she knew at Central, but there was no reason on earth to cry poor mouth all the time, either.

Behind the cash register, Paul read the morning *Free Press*, the only chance he'd had to look at it all day. With color washed out of his face and his jaw sagging slightly open from fatigue, everything in his body seemed to be pulled downward. A stranger might guess him closer to middle age than his twenty-nine years. Maybe he was worried about running the diner without her. Thelma tried to push the notion out of her head. She realized for the first time how much he was beginning to look like their father; she imagined him shrinking, growing gray, opening his belt buckle a notch. Paul is going to die one day, she said to herself; and the truth of it twisted her heart so, she had to squeeze her eyes shut a moment to blot out the knowing.

Paul was twelve years older than she was; Thelma, her mother had informed her more than once, had been an "accident." They were close, she and Paul, despite the difference in their ages. He still called her his baby sister sometimes; she used to say she would marry him when she grew up. As far back as she could remember, he had told her stories of how it would be when they had enough money to move out of their parents' house and into a little place for themselves.

"Do you know what the front room furniture actually looks like?" he had asked her once. "Have you ever touched the material? The God damned davenport hasn't seen daylight in so many years, it would crumble like an Egyptian mummy if it ever got exposed to air." He ground out a cigarette and said, "I swear, Thelma, if they could slip cover *us* they'd do it . . . save on soap and water."

Paul did move out, but he didn't take Thelma with him. After a couple of years at Wayne University, he joined the army, and when he came home on leave in his uniform, he looked too big for the house, as if the scale of things had been reduced and he no longer fit. He went away again, sent home glittering, hand-painted souvenir pillows from God knows where and boxes of chocolates, stale by the time they arrived. He left the army, hitch-hiked across the country; Thelma lost track. Then one day he came home . . . "For good," he said. He had gotten it out of his system, whatever "it" was. He cashed in his war bonds and made a down payment on the diner at Linwood and Davison in Detroit.

Thelma remembered the night Paul moved back into the house, a radio under his arm, a heavy khaki duffle bag in one hand, a leather valise in the other. He had stood in the doorway and shouted, "Okay, folks, whip out the fatted calf; the prodigal son is re-turned!"

Throwing down the book she was reading, Thelma had rushed down the stairs and into his arms. "Fatted calf," she said. "Har de har har."

Now Thelma glanced up as a grizzled old man lowered himself stiffly onto a stool and pretended to study the typed menu. Poor old Jonathan Bing. Arms folded across her chest, Thelma waited, depressed by his Goodwill overcoat draped over his shoulders as though hung on a hook and fashioned of some name-less material that might have been cardboard. Another victim, she told herself.

At last, he asked if he might have two pieces of toast. She prompted him, not unkindly, "And a cup of hot water, right?"

He looked at her, uncertain of her tone, and then, evidently deciding he could not afford the luxury of nuance, said, "Please."

Jesus Christ, Thelma thought. At this rate, Paul and I can join him on the street. Still, she slid the catsup bottle down the counter and tried not to stare at the old guy as he slapped the bottle over the cup of water with the flat of his hand.

My face, I don't mind it . . . Paul had taught her that rhyme when she first became aware that her nose wasn't going to stop growing just because she prayed it would. Thelma formed a steeple with her two index fingers and then ran the fingers down the sides of her nose. The shape was so familiar to her. She wondered if she would always feel it the way it was now even after she had the other nose. Would the Thelma in her dreams still bear the old nose? *My face I don't mind it, because I'm behind it . . .* She had an impulse to discuss the question with the surgeon, ask him for the pieces of excess flesh and cartilage so that she might bury them in a proper ceremony. She shook her head. People didn't do crazy things like that. And her fingers would always shape themselves to the old dimensions; she was certain of it.

Thelma popped up the two slices of Tip Top bread, slapped on melted butter with a basting brush, and, placing them on a plate, handed them gently to the old man. Her kindness was deliberate; in fact he gave her the creeps. Her friend, Eugene, accused her of loving humanity in the abstract. "When they start to sweat, you check out," he said. Years before, she had seen an old man like this one peeing in an alley, had seen a thing hang out of his unbuttoned pants she thought were his intestines. The pink and gray mass figured in her dreams for a long time, but she didn't tell anyone about it, not even Paul, sensing that she had stumbled into a place where she was a stranger, where she did not want to claim citizenship.

Paul was still on the road the first time Thelma approached her mother about the operation. She was fifteen that September, and school had started. Not a good time to talk of money, with her mother in a decline because of added expenses for the Jewish holidays. That fall, several students came back from summer vacation with names and noses bobbed. To Thelma they seemed to float in a privileged aura, cut loose from unwanted flesh and syllables. I'm not stuck forever, Thelma told herself. It is possible for things to change.

"Where will the money come for this *mishegoss?*" Thelma's mother whined. "Who do you think your father is . . . John D. Rockefeller?" She stood at the gas range, frying chicken hearts, and the sour stink hung blue in the kitchen. Through a hole cut out with a razor blade in her mother's felt slippers, Thelma could see a gnarled, yellow corn. Too cheap to go to a foot doctor.

"Ma," Thelma said, knowing it was hopeless, "I'll pay you back . . ."

Her mother interrupted. "Pay me back," she mocked. "With what . . . your big inheritance? Besides," she said, triumphantly, "*God* gave you the nose."

"God?" Thelma lashed out, "You don't even believe in God!" Still, she didn't say, "I'll die," the way another girl might. Sometimes she thought that was what her mother wanted to hear.

Instead, she began saving money, squirreling it away in a Swee Touch Nee tea box that she hid on one of the rafters in the attic. At first she saved without a fixed goal in mind, afraid to find out what the surgery cost for fear she would get discouraged and quit. She practiced economies even her own mother hadn't the wit to dream of, giving up movies, records, candy bars. Her body grew scrawny from skipped lunches. Only her nose in that pinched, white face seemed larger than ever.

Early in the year that she turned sixteen, a young couple who lived in Russell Woods, a new Jewish neighborhood, hired Thelma to baby-sit for them several times a week. Their eldest child, a little boy in yellow Dr. Denton's, was galloping around the living room the first time Thelma met him. Out of a picture book, she thought, admiring his brown curls, the fringed lashes, the blood-red mouth, and button nose.

Baby was in her crib, Mrs. Sandow told Thelma, and would probably sleep through if Brian didn't wake her. "Show Thelma your cowboy hat and holster, Brian," she said and let herself out the front door, a sweet-faced young woman in a green suit. Mr. Sandow waited on the side drive, the Pontiac's motor running as if for a quick getaway.

After Thelma shut Brian's door for the tenth (and last) time she told him, she tip-toed down the hall to listen for Baby. The crib, in shadow, stood across the room from where a night light glowed dimly in a baseboard socket. The bed was empty, or so it appeared to Thelma, and for one split second, she felt her heart leap like a flushed bird. Then she spotted the small curly-topped bundle wedged into a corner of the crib. Beautiful like Brian, Thelma told herself and crept farther into the room, feeling just a bit foolish for having been so frightened. Baby slept on her back. Thelma put her face so close she could smell Johnson's powder and the warm, milky scent from the child's mouth.

When her eyes grew adjusted to the half-light, Thelma could make out a dresser and a clown lamp, a rocking chair, and stuffed toys. Then she looked back down at Baby. What slept there was Brian's face, but each feature seemed to have been tormented into a perverse distortion of what should have been. "Oh, Honey," she whispered, trying to swallow her horror. She started as the violet eyelids fluttered, then stared at the pulled-down eye socket, the flattened nose, the tiny mouth twisted into a snarl. For a long time, Thelma stood quietly, holding Baby's foot, feeling the rubbery bones through the soft flannel. A feeling of love, more passionate than any she had ever experienced before surged through her. "Honey, Honey," she said, again and again.

Thelma would have died before asking the Sandows what had happened to the infant. Her own theory was that Baby simply had not wanted to be born, and in the ensuing struggle lost both the battle and her face. At night, Thelma's sleep was often plagued by recurring dreams in which Baby appeared. She could never remember the preliminaries, but each time she would find herself stuffing the child, battered head first, down a well or a toilet, and always she could hear Baby crying long after her mouth was underwater.

When both children were asleep, Thelma foraged

for food, so hungry she gnawed the cold steak bones on the dinner plates the Sandows left for her to wash. The food! Thelma had never seen anything like it. Whole salamis hung to dry from hooks in the kitchen. Bowls of fruit bloomed everywhere, overflowing with grapes and ripe plums, even in winter. She opened the refrigerator over and over just to look at the packages from the deli: sliced swiss and meunster, lox, cream cheese, halvah—all in their oily, white wrappers. Cans of Del Monte tuna, Pillar Rock salmon, and brisling sardines, purchased by the dozen and stacked in pyramids, resembled the lavish displays of a grocery rather than a kitchen cupboard.

Salted almonds, walnuts, and cashews sat openly in little silver dishes on every table in the living and dining rooms where anyone could grab a handful. The Sandows kept a special tin of candy called Almond Roca on the dining room buffet. Each time she babysat, Thelma took one piece, praying they did not count the candies as her mother would have done had she ever bought anything so frivolous.

Thelma combed the Sandow's library, puzzled and excited by the kind of books she had never seen before except under lock and key in the adult section behind the librarian's desk at the Parkman Branch. She read *Tropic of Cancer* and *Tropic of Capricorn* in their French paper covers and *Studs Lonigan* and Joyce's *Ulysses*. A small shelf in the Sandow's bedroom held writings of Freud, Kraft-Ebbing, and Jung. She found colored

pictures of male and female sexual organs and illustrations of sexual positions she had never imagined
and would have thought illegal if she had. One book
contained reproductions of paintings in which oriental
men and women curled about one another so intri-
cately, she could not tell which limbs belonged to what
person. On the Sandow's bedside table, between leather
book ends, stood a set of two volumes called *Frigidity
in Women*. Thelma read those, too.

The rich food and the memory of the books agitated
her so much that sometimes she was unable to sleep
when she got into bed at night. She would try to think
of Frank Sinatra then, shy and vulnerable looking,
with that little curl in his voice that made her insides
shiver. But as hard as she tried to blot it out, Baby's
crumpled face would mix itself up with her thoughts.
She would picture the oriental figures coiling like vines
and the old man with his pink and gray intestines
hanging out of his pants. In her mouth she felt the
shape of green grapes, broken from heavy clusters,
their skin at room temperature making her gag as if
she were consuming human flesh. Then she would
give up sleep and sit in a chair by the window over
the street. She had no boyfriend for a long time. The
nose was her excuse.

Sandow didn't seem to mind her nose. When he
drove her home late at night, he twirled the steering
wheel expertly in one hand, and no matter how far
away from him Thelma sat, he managed to touch her

knee every time he shifted gears. Sometimes he rested his hand on the seat between them so it casually lay against her thigh. She could feel the warmth of his fingers through her skirt, and her skin recoiled. Sandow should read something besides all those sex books, she told herself. Then he wouldn't be so hard up all the time.

Thelma wondered if Mrs. Sandow knew what her husband did with baby sitters. Perhaps, being frigid, she was happy to have his attention elsewhere. Thelma was certain Mrs. Sandow was frigid. Why else keep those particular books where they could be referred to without even getting out of bed. Maybe she was frigid because she feared another freak like Baby. Poor Baby. Poor everyone. Mostly Thelma wished Sandow would leave her alone. That thin little mustache and kinky hair . . . She shuddered, but the money was growing in the tea box, and she didn't want to do or say anything to risk her job.

Lifting the heavy dishpan, Thelma set it in the sink. All that was a long time ago. She had been to the plastic surgeon, had seen the before and after pictures in a loose-leaf folder in his office, had sat patiently through his lecture warning her not to expect her life to change because she was losing a few scraps of flesh and bone. What do you know about it, Thelma thought, and the jingle started in her head again. *My face, I don't mind it, because I'm behind it* . . . She rinsed the soapy dishes, one by one, in scalding water. It was almost over, the grinding hours in the diner, the permanent slip of grease between her fingers, the counting . . . the counting.

Tomorrow afternoon she would be checking into the hospital; in a week or two, a new Thelma would emerge from behind the gauze. Why didn't she feel more elation then? She had fastened her sights on the sum for so long, only the money seemed real. The image of the red tea-tin, empty, raped of its contents, filled her with foreboding. For a moment, she had a vision of the future: the operation over, her life no different—only the tea box with nothing inside for her to fondle.

Paul turned back the black-and-white sign so that "closed" faced outside. Then he pulled down the window shade. "Sorry, Pop," he said to the old man. "I know it's cold out there."

Thelma sighed. The sign got to her. Symbols everywhere. OPEN/CLOSED. She was closed—like a fist, like an early flower. She was closing the door on the long, sometimes terrible, first part of her life. Starting tomorrow . . . What? She saw the coming years as if they lay waiting for her across an ocean of speculation: America, wild, green, and undiscovered, opening to her grudgingly, one perilous step at a time. Well, it wasn't tomorrow yet. She still had one more bit of business to take care of.

From the far end of the counter, Thelma watched the old man spill sugar onto a napkin, twist the paper, and put it into his pocket. There's poor and then there's really poor, she thought. Hunching his shoulders in the thin coat, the man shuffled out the door, almost bumping into Eugene as he did. Thelma's hand flew to her nose. She cupped her palm over it as though she were scratching the side. Then, aware of what she had just done, she deliberately pulled her hand away. "Shalom," she said, taking a deep drag on her cigarette, so the smoke hung in the air for a moment before she dragged it down her lungs. "I was ready to give you up." Eugene smiled. He never made excuses. That was his style.

Eugene Victor, he was. Named for Debs, he told her when they met, but his friends called him "Lenny." "Tell me about the rabbits, George." The year before, Thelma had joined a Labor Zionist group because she hoped Socialists might not feel ugly noses mattered the way bourgeois people did. She and her friend, Norma, stood outside the labor Zionist Institute on Linwood a dozen times reading the "Everyone Welcome" sign before they trusted it enough to go in one night. Thelma spotted Eugene right away; he was the biggest young man she had ever seen.

Norma stopped coming, but Thelma went to meetings whenever she would allow herself a few hours off from the diner. After a while, she felt comfortable enough to join in the political arguments and the discussions of books. She loved the feeling of flying when she circled the room in a hora, Eugene's hand swallowing hers, his lumbering thigh banging against her hip. Noses didn't count, he told her, only a person's essence. Thelma wished for a beautiful essence *and* a beautiful nose. Now Eugene spoke gravely of going off to Israel when he turned eighteen to fight for the creation of a Jewish state. That kind of talk made Thelma sad. She felt she was suddenly losing too many things.

"Paul, I told Ma I was sleeping at Doris's house," Thelma shouted from the rest room where she was changing out of her white uniform. When she came out, dressed in heavy sweater, khaki pants, and an army jacket, the uniform of the movement, she said, "I'll call you tomorrow . . . early." It was hard, making it all sound casual. She had never spent the night at Eugene's before.

"What's that all about?" Eugene asked. "Aren't you working tomorrow?"

"I'll tell you about it later," Thelma replied, wondering if she would. On the papers she had filled out at the surgeon's office, Thelma had put Paul's name after "next of kin." No one else knew about the operation, not her parents, not even Eugene. The Eugene part bothered her; she was not sure how he would feel about something as materialistic as a nose job.

At the register, Paul counted change into a canvas bag. "There's coffee left in the urn, Eugene," he said. "It could wake a dead man. You wanna cup?"

He doesn't want us to go, Thelma realized, but Eugene shook his head.

"You wanna doughnut or a candy bar for the road?"

"That's okay, Paul," she said.

"Thelma," he began again. Eugene was gripping her shoulder. If Paul says "baby sister," I won't be able to take it, she told herself. Instead, he slammed the cash register shut.

"I'll talk to you tomorrow," he said firmly. And then, "Take care." That was it.

Linwood was quiet. In an all-night deli, a customer or two drowsed over warmed-up coffee; a lone man waited at the prescription counter of Hammerstein's Drugs. Even the Linwood Theater was dark, the last half of the double feature rewound and in the can. Thelma shivered. Overhead, thickly sprinkled stars glittered like mica on a movie placard. "It's zero," she said, peering at an outdoor thermometer hung on a hardware store window. Eugene said nothing, but he gripped her more firmly about the shoulders.

Thelma whispered, "I'm scared, Eugene; don't you sometimes feel like everything's coming to an end? I do. Like pretty soon they'll make me put it all away: the baggy jeans, army pants and big shirts, and the curse words and straight hair, hanging long and free. I don't want to lose it, Eugene, the days when it goes right, and we all sit around the table at Paul and Sid's singing 'Red River Valley' and 'Raise the Scarlet Banner,' and you can feel the older people at other tables envying how young we are and wishing they had in on our sweet communion."

She pulled away from the weight of his arm on her

shoulders and looked at him curiously, feeling for once, that they were equals, that his silence proved he was frightened, too, that for once, her need of him was no stronger than his for her. Let's get it over with now, she told herself, first the one and then the other.

Eugene unlocked the front door, and they walked in on exaggerated tiptoe, nervously giggling, even though his parents were visiting relatives in Cleveland and planned to be away for the weekend. Before he turned on the lights, Eugene carefully pulled down the shades in the living room while Thelma waited in the front hall. Clearing his throat, Eugene said, "Want something to eat?"

He's stalling, thought Thelma, maybe it's *his* first time, too. She began to unbutton her jacket. "What do you say we take our coats off first," she suggested.

Eugene's bedroom was large, carpeted, and neat. Thelma noticed a football, packs of baseball cards separated by rubber bands, a Detroit Tigers pennant on the wall, a record player and classical records lined up against another wall. The tidiness surprised her; Eugene's size seemed to go with records gathering dust on turntables and single socks under the bed. Being in his room turned her suddenly silent and shy, as if she had walked in on an intimate conversation between strangers or a party to which she had not been invited.

Eugene crossed his arms in front of himself and pulled his undershirt over his head. Washboard belly self-consciously sucked in, he stood across the room from her, his caramel colored chest as smooth and hairless as her own. Thelma wondered what she would do for a nightgown, whether she would have the nerve to undress in front of him, whether her mother would need to get in touch with her and would call her at Doris's house. In her imagination, this scene had all taken place under the covers; she hadn't reckoned with the stunning shyness of preliminaries. "Where's the john?" she asked finally, "I have to go." Opening a dresser drawer, Eugene handed her a pyjama top and pointed the way. He seemed relieved to have something to do.

Thelma undressed in the bathroom, catching glimpses of her flushed face in the mirror over the sink as she pulled off her sweater, stepped out of her pants. *My face, I don't mind it* . . . She shook the rhyme out of her head. Reaching behind her back, she unhooked her bra and let it slip down her arms. Her breasts were full, uptilted, her waist slender. Put a bag over my head, and I'd do, she thought. She could feel her legs tremble as if they might give way. You've just been on your feet too long today, she told herself. Stop making such a big deal out of everything.

Quietly she checked the door to make certain she had locked it, and then sat on the toilet, flushing it quickly, ashamed of the sound her own water made; Thelma wondered if people overcame their inhibitions when they got married. Once she opened the bathroom door by mistake when her father was in the tub, and she saw her mother sitting on the toilet lid arguing with him. Thelma had been so shocked to find them both in the bathroom at the same time that for a long while afterward she believed she had imagined the scene.

Now she wished she had thought to bring a toothbrush, but she couldn't bring herself to use one of the several brightly colored brushes that poked into a holder near the sink. Now *you* stop stalling, she said, this is it. For a moment, she considered getting dressed again and walking out the front door. She decided she didn't have the energy for all the explanations that would have to follow. She could tell him her period had just started and she had cramps; then she could just sleep by herself on the couch in the living room. But what she had planned to do had to be done by the old Thelma. Perhaps her essence wouldn't change tomorrow, but everything else would . . . she knew it. And so, she scrubbed herself hard with a washcloth, put on the pajama top, and unlocked the door.

Eugene, chest bare, lay half-covered, his back to the wall. A reproduction of a painting of a factory worker, welder's mask tipped up on his head, hung behind him. Diego Rivera's mural in the Detroit Institute of Arts. "I have a prophylactic," Eugene told her. "It's my dad's."

Does getting it from your father make it more legal or less? Thelma wondered. Actually she was surprised at how little she felt now, not fear, not anticipation, not even curiosity. The boy in bed might have been a stranger . . . Lenny. Lifting the blanket—a white Hudson's Bay with red and green and yellow stripes—she slid in beside him, shocked at the connection of cold sheets and bare flesh. "Oh," she said, reaching for him, "warm my bones!" They rolled on the bed, over and over.

Thelma closed her eyes and clenched her teeth. Eugene was everywhere, at her mouth, her earlobes, her breasts. The bed shook with his heaving and she, suddenly seasick, said, "Wait, my arm! You're smashing it." After a moment, the rolling began again. Once she caught sight of his erect penis, like the stalk of an exotic plant. Sandow's books, she said to herself. Sandow with his skinny mustache, the pink and gray "intestines," Baby's tormented face. She could hear Eugene make a ripping sound in his chest, like her father's saw when it first bit into a plank.

"Give me the rubber," Eugene said. "Quick! There on the table . . ."

Thelma said, "Wait," but it was too late. It was all over. Eugene's body heaved once more and lay still.

Afterward, they changed the sheets, and Eugene threw the soiled ones into the washing machine. His skin had a greenish cast, like brass turning. For someone who had an opinion about everything, he had been uncharacteristically quiet all evening. Now he wanted to talk. "I don't know what happened," he said, shaking his head. "It was probably a mistake to use my father's . . ." Then he remembered that he didn't make excuses.

"It's no big deal," Thelma told him. "It's really okay, and anyway the rest of it was really good for me." She touched his arm. "Was it good for you, too?"

Barefoot, they stood on the cold cement floor of the basement, watching the sheets bob up and down in the Maytag. Would she have to lie like that with the new nose? Thelma didn't know. For that matter, why the fuss over a bit of excess flesh? Her life lay ahead of her; there was time enough for all the losses that would certainly ensue whether she willed them or not. She put her hand up to her face, grateful for the familiar dimensions for just a little longer.

The Change

ONE MORE WEEK'S SHOPPING and she would have a complete set, (service for eight) of the Oneida flatware A&P had been offering all spring with each seven dollar and fifty cent purchase. Just in time, too; she and Connor were always ending up with five cups and six saucers or not enough dinner plates. Her cupboards were filled with uneven sets of dishes and odd glasses from the Shell Station bonus, of the State Theater dish night, or a supermarket special offer. Somehow the giveaways seemed to end before they ever collected a complete set of anything. Cora remembered she was thinking that the first time Connor talked to her about the girl moving in. Funny how you carry unimportant things along with the important ones because that was also the night the whole business began with her body.

They had been sitting in the kitchen having supper when he brought up the subject of the girl. She remembered afterward that he took his own sweet time of it, too. The dirty dishes, pools of grease hardening on them, were stacked in the sink and he had pushed his chrome and vinyl chair back, was in fact, rocking on its hind legs, his pants unbuttoned, zipper forced half-way open by the belly he had put on.

"Honey," (he said "haw-ney") "wait on the dishes for a minute."

She had begun to gather the remaining cutlery and the saucers from which they had eaten chocolate ice cream.

"What's the matter?"

She knew his "Honey," knew he was up to something when he drew that first syllable out as though it were a rope of taffy.

"Nothin's the matter. Does it have to be something the matter for us to sit a minute after supper and talk?"

Nevertheless, she stood up, holding the sauce dishes in one hand and the spoons in the other. "Well, I can tell something's the matter by the foolish look on your face."

She poured boiling water from the tea kettle into the stoppered sink, and carefully submerged the scraped dishes. Then she turned to him again, still standing, a dish towel under her arm. He rocked forward and brushed a crumb from the oilcloth covered table top into his cupped palm. Oh, didn't she know how to read the signs when he wanted something? He looked down at the oilcloth and with a blunt thumbnail traced around the design of a pear on the table cover.

"You know that girl up to Kilby's?"

"Of course I know that girl up to Kilby's. And what about her? The pants factory's full of it. Can't hardly do your work for the gossip about it."

Cora pulled out her chair and sat sideways on it. She didn't like that butter-wouldn't-melt-in-his-mouth tone, couldn't quite figure it out. She thought she knew him inside out. The rages she could handle, or had to, but he was getting at her a different way this time.

"I've been thinking, Cora," he said, carefully. "The girl can't stay at Kilby's what with the talk and all, and she ain't got no place to go. Now, I been figurin' on helpin' Kilby out."

"Oh, you been figurin' on helpin' Kilby out!"

"Well, yes I have, and don't you be mockin' every word I say."

"What's she got to do with us. She ain't no kin of ours. She's Ella's niece, not Kilby's. *Kilby's* your cousin."

"Now I know that, Cora," he said as though he were talking to a child or someone whose brains were addled. "But you know how worn out you are these days, what with workin' and all. Maybe we could take her off Kilby's hands, let her stay here and help with the house and the garden and all." He looked at her and then plunged ahead in spite of what he saw on her face. "We never should have lost all them beans or them tomatoes, either. You could come home from the pants factory and there'd be supper on the table, and you sittin' there like the queen of England on TV."

He kept right on going: B'rer Rabbit, sticking another limb on to that tar baby, and she flew at him, would have pecked his eyes out if she had had a beak.

"Well, what about them tomatoes and beans? You fixin' to feed the county this winter? There ain't but two of us the last time I counted."

Connor hunched his squat shoulders over the table and waved an arm at her. "Well, nobody ever could have a simple conversation with you. Go jumpin' around like water on a hot griddle." She felt it then for the first time, a surge of fire in her as though her very veins were like the coils of the heater they used in the winter on extra cold nights. The heat seemed to radiate red-hot for thirty seconds or so and then cut off, leaving her dripping with a cold sweat.

"I think I'm feverish," she said, fanning herself with the dish towel, and moments later, shivering, "I like to catch my death."

"Now Cora, that's just what I mean. If Kilby's girl was here, you could go to bed right now, and *she'd* do the dishes.

"I can do my own dishes, thank you very much." She turned to the sink, giving him her back, plunging her hands into the still scalding water, glad of the warmth. She poured boiling water over each dish as she mopped it, skillfully hoarding the water so he would not have to go outside and fetch her another bucket from the pump. How many years had he promised to pipe water into the house? *That* would save her some steps.

Stacking the plates in the dish drainer, she thought to herself that Connor wasn't about to give up. Stubborn . . . he could give a mule a run for its money.

"Now you know it ain't her fault Kilby's after her. And it ain't like we don't have the room."

Oh, they had the room alright. Connor had built this house shortly after they were married, when things were slack during the Depression. Mr. and Mrs. Jenkins had done their best, but she never felt quite easy, living in their house. Even though she and Connor would wait until his parents were in bed, she had to beg him each night to go easy so they wouldn't wake her in-laws with their rattling. The very idea of it still made her color rise. Not that they'd done a lot of good with all that racket.

Cora shook Ajax into the sink and scoured the porcelain with a dishrag. And the way Mr. Jenkins had treated Connor: that was hard to take. Hiring that colored boy to help with the calving when money was so scarce. Couldn't have cut Connor better if he had used a knife. Not that they hadn't always treated Connor like dirt. Singled him out from the start the way people do some kids. The old man was always beating on him when he was a boy; Connor had told her that; he had no sense about embarrassing his son in front of a young wife, either. Never did let him forget about that newborn calf falling over and breaking its neck. Now what could anyone have done about that? Didn't notice the colored boy doing anything about saving it. Connor'd hunted all night for the cow . . . had followed the bellowing up the mountain. Whose fault was it the sorry thing had caught her leg in a fallen tree limb and couldn't get it untangled? Whose fault was it that the calf had been born before Connor could get to them? Head so big it couldn't keep it up. And the old man, close to ninety now, still bringing it up every chance he got.

"Connor," she said, more softly, "I ain't takin' no sixteen-year-old girl into this house. It just don't make no sense to me."

He scraped his chair back abruptly and went out the back door to the shop behind the house. In a few minutes, she could hear the whine of the power saw. She stood up, closed the light in the kitchen, and walked into the living room. They get crazy this time of life, she thought. They get thoughts, and no one can talk them out of them. Now what would they want to take that girl in for? It was all over the county that Kilby couldn't keep his hands off her. Sorry old thing . . . old enough to be her father twice, but she'd heard of things like that before. Down at the pants

factory . . . talk of Mary Lee Fincham's husband taking off after his own daughter-in-law. Everyone knew
about it. Started in gabbing about it the minute Mary
Lee went on relief. Funny thing was she didn't really
blame Connor.

She had thoughts, too. Kilby's girl reminded her of
the yellow Easter cups that grew early in spring; her
hair was that pale gold color they hid deep inside.
When she and Connor went to Kilby's, Cora found
reasons to stay in the place where the girl was. She
couldn't get too much of the sweet little titties plump-
ing out the thin cotton T-shirts she always wore. Cora
had to remind herself not to stare at the place below
the girl's small waist where tight blue jeans outlined
a perfect triangle like a fat wedge of layer cake. Such
a pretty thing.

Cora sat down in front of the darkened TV set. No
one to talk to about any of it, of course, even if she
dared. Mama had her hands full these days, what with
Daddy taking on so. It was a pity to watch him. Last
Sunday when they had gone to visit, he'd carried on
something terrible, hollering "Take me home, Ada,
take me home." Mama had the patience of a saint,
though. There he was trampling all through that bit
of corn he'd managed to put in, and Mama had got
him in the house and calmed him, even managed to
talk him into eating some supper. He seemed right,
too, for a while . . . mind clear as a bell, talking about
hay prices and the drought and all. And then he'd

looked up at Mama, sitting right there at the table and he'd said, "Ada, who are these strangers? Get the wagon and take me home." And Mama had said, "Why Mr. Yates, you old fool, you *are* home, and this is your very own daughter, Cora, and her husband, Connor. Now stop worrying me to death, and eat your supper I fixed you."

Now there was Connor worrying *her* to death, sawing away out there as if he'd never stop. She knew how stubborn he always was; he'd wear himself out and then fall asleep on that little cot he kept out there. Well, good! Let him keep the sawdust out of the house until morning. Time enough to clean it up then.

Their bedroom was small, hardly room in it for the wardrobe closet Connor had built and their bed, so she took her clothes off in the front room. Out of habit, she undressed under her nightgown, even though Connor was not there to look at her. She supposed it would have been better if she had not always been so shy about herself, and wondered why she was thinking about that now. If she had been able to bring herself to let a doctor look at her down there, she might not be fussing with Connor now about an empty spare room.

The bed sheets were damp-cold, like the underbelly of a frog. Virginia fall nights ate into your bones . . . pneumonia weather. She crawled out of bed. Should have gone out back before, but she didn't want to run into Connor . . . hated to use the slop jar. She pulled the china pot from under the bed, removed the lid and squatted over it drowsily. Nothing to wipe herself with . . . paper napkins in the kitchen. Once more under the covers she allowed herself to do that thing with her fingers she had discovered by accident long ago . . . nobody to see her tonight. Probably a sin, but wasn't everything? It was a long while before she fell asleep.

And when she did sleep, she dreamed uneasily, and, as usual, the whir of the sewing machines droned in her head. Thick bolts of yard goods unwound themselves, billowing sails of red, blue, and yellow. As her body turned like a spindle, soft checks, stripes, flowers, grew around her, yard after yard, always the same: binding first her feet together, then her arms fast to her sides, and finally, the lovely fabrics spiraling around her head as if they were winding sheets, choking her in the stifling, starchy scent of her own desire.

Connor was quiet the next morning at breakfast, but then he was always pulled into himself when he first got up. Seemed like it took him most of the day to come far out enough to talk to people, even her. Cora shook oatmeal into a big pot of boiling water, and when it was cooked, they both ate silently. He needed his strength, fencing, mowing, walking his legs off all over creation, and as for her, there didn't seem to be a way to fill her up lately. They were both doctoring for high blood, but she sliced off a generous pat of butter, anyway, and let it melt in the cereal before she spooned on sugar and poured on cream.

Funny thing was, the rolls of fat still surprised her; she had been a slim girl once and could not really believe how stout she had become. She rarely saw herself naked, ordered her dresses from the Ward's catalogue, and they owned no full-length mirror. In the employee's washroom at work, she tried to avoid looking into the glass. If she thought about it, she would have said she long ago gave up caring about the way she looked, yet in her purse, she carried a sepia snapshot of herself, slender in a white dress and patent leather shoes, pretty as a movie star. She took it out and looked at it sometimes.

Connor dropped her off at work at five till seven, leaving her at the entrance of the pants factory where she'd worked ever since the Second World War. Connor had had a farm deferment during the war and then had worked road construction for the state, but he never could stay long with anybody. What happened was he kept quarreling with the supervisors, complained they didn't talk to him right, or that they wouldn't listen to his ideas . . . always said he did the work faster and better than the rest of the guys and nobody would ever give him credit for it.

Times were easier now that the city people were buying up the old farms. Those people respected Connor, would listen to him when he gave them advice. Strange that, as unhappy as he had been in the old days, he still kept telling the city folks how much better life was then. Even his father: much as they hadn't gotten along, she noticed how often he mentioned things Mr. Jenkins had said, and how many times Connor would tell people how right his daddy had been about this or that. Like that sign tacked up over the cash register at the Boston store: "Just when you're old enough to realize your parents weren't wrong about everything, your children are old enough to realize you are."

She slouched over her sewing machine, sewing zipper after zipper into its own smooth placket. She could have done it in her sleep . . . did it in her sleep . . . was warned against it: "Keep awake for safety's sake!" Her mind skittered here, there, no way to fasten on anything. Thoughts—crazy, fly-away threads thrown out with no center around which to revolve. Thoughts cut loose, maintaining out of habit, their circular pattern at first, then, in ever-widening loops, forgetting design, snaring her in their tangles.

After work, Connor picked her up, and they shopped at A&P. She wheeled her cart through the crowded aisles buying soft, white bread, four loaves for a dollar; pale, pink baloney; and marbled headcheese for sandwiches. She took down marshmallow cookies and jars of processed cheese spread, peanut butter and canned peaches. At the checkout counter, she asked for her dinner fork. Mrs. Carpenter's boy, Scotty, told her they were sold out of them, and no, he didn't know if they'd get anymore in.

When the groceries were packed in the camper top

of the pickup, Connor took her to McDonald's. Lately they ate out often on Friday nights. Things weren't so tight as they had been, what with the extra money from the city people. Cora sat at the little yellow plastic table, eating the soft food dreamily. They didn't talk. She sucked the sweet, cold milkshake up her straw. The girl wasn't mentioned. Once she shook off the sweater she wore round her shoulders and said, "My, it's hot in here. Ain't you hot, Connor, in that jacket?" She didn't wait for his answer because in a few moments, she was chilled enough to put her arms through the sweater's sleeves and button it all the way down.

Saturday night, they went to Bob's Auction House. Connor liked to see what price people were willing to give for what he called "local trash." He never bought anything. He just liked to sit there on the reclaimed movie theater seats telling her how much the buyers were getting cheated. "Now you take that chair over there," he would say into her ear, "he calls it an *an-tique*; I call it a piece of junk somebody left out in the rain for two-three years."

Cora looked around her in the drafty shed where they sat facing the raised platform that served as a display area for the furniture, tools, and glassware to be auctioned, and as a kind of stage for "Colonel" Bob Reese to put on his show. "Now what am I bid for a little outfit like this," he was saying, holding up an electric percolator with its cord missing. "Owner says it was working when he brought it in here."

It all made Cora so tired . . . those dusty cardboard

boxes of mismatched dishes and battered pans, the heavy oak furniture she had grown up with that city people now bid up to crazy prices. She couldn't understand why they wanted it all when the same money could buy shining new pots and the lovely blonde woods she saw in the furniture stores and coveted so.

Besides, going to the auction was like going anyplace else with Connor: there were always so many people she had to pass by and pretend she didn't see. There were Lloyd and Wilma Hinkler, for instance. She couldn't speak with them, even though Wilma was her cousin, because Connor had had words with Lloyd about a fence they shared. There was Walter Strether, another neighbor. She had to lower her eyes when she saw him, too. He and Connor had argued about Walter wanting to charge them for letting their cow be with his bull. "Daddy let him have that favor for years and never let him pay a cent," Connor had raged. "Now let him wait till he needs something from *me.*" A woman had to stick by her man, Cora knew that. They even sang about it on the radio, but she still didn't like it. One day there wouldn't be anybody left in the county they could talk with, and then what would they do?

Kilby and Ella came in, sliding across the knees of people in the row ahead of her. Cora saw that the girl was with them, following sullenly behind Ella, her long hair the color of a hay rick, her waist so tiny it seemed a bracelet could have been clasped around it.

Cora could smell her perfume, lily of the valley, recognized from years back when she had snatched dabs of it from the little bottles she had unstoppered in the dime store. She fanned herself with her handkerchief. So many people always made a place feel close, especially in the fall when doors were kept shut against the chill.

Connor had his reading glasses stuck on the end of his nose. He was puzzling out the words on one of the circulars Col. Bob's daughter had handed them when they walked in. At home Cora would have read it to him, as she read to him directions on boxes of medicine and bottles of insect spray, as she read to him the few letters or bills that were ever placed in their mailbox at the road. It wasn't his fault that he had been pulled out of school at the end of fifth grade. His daddy needed him on the farm, and what did a boy who was going to be a farmer need with schooling anyway? She had gone on to tenth grade, had dreamed of being a bookkeeper; she was so good with numbers. Kilby's girl pushed her way back across the bent knees and walked toward the door. Two round sugar loaves in those tight pants. Poor Ella.

Col. Bob's voice crackled over the hand microphone he carried, and in front of him the audience chatted to one another, a sound rising from them like the brooding of chickens. Connor brought Cora a ham biscuit and sweet coffee and a slab of coconut cake from the refreshment stand in the entry. She ate slowly, enjoying the treats, the cackling and brooding melting to gibberish in her ears.

Kilby's girl came back, carrying a little green bottle of Coke in her hand. Cora could see a ring with a blue stone on one of the girl's thin fingers. Cora had had to have her own wedding band cut from her finger when the flesh grew around it and threatened to stop her circulation. That was a long time ago. Now she saw the girl whisper in Kilby's ear and point with the Coke bottle to a place behind Col. Bob. Cora wondered why she hadn't seen it before, that picture hanging on the wall. It was framed in golden painted wood, a picture of autumn leaves turning color just like they did every year, all gold and red and brown. Nothing else was in the picture, no animals or people that she could see, just a smooth dirt path, wide at the front of the painting and cleverly narrowing as it led back into the dark woods and disappeared in shadow.

She didn't tell Connor that she wanted it, just didn't need to have him start in about getting cheated and all. She told him she had to go to the toilet, went out front, signed her name, Cora Jenkins, Boston, Virginia, and came back with her own card, number 54, good luck she thought because by coincidence it was her exact age. She slipped the card into her pocketbook trembling just a little; she had never done anything like that before.

Nine-thirty came and Col. Bob still hadn't come to the picture, and Cora was beside herself with worry that he had forgotten it. It didn't seem strange to her

118

that half an hour ago she hadn't even known the picture was there and now she felt as though everything she had ever longed for was wrapped up in it. A hundred times she ran her eyes over the buttery curlicues and gilded flowers decorating the frame. At least a dozen times she said to herself that she knew exactly where to put it, on the wall away from the wood stove so it wouldn't get smoked up so quickly. The colors would go with the new yellow-and-brown linoleum rug Connor had put down this spring. She could look at the picture all winter when the real leaves were trampled to black earth underfoot.

People were leaving now, turning in their numbers, paying for the few things they had bought. Several red-faced, tight-lipped women, one of whom she worked with, followed men carrying boxes of broken irons, toasters that didn't heat, and radios that didn't play—more excuses to keep them from work they should have been doing. Connor stood up and leaned against a back wall. The pace had picked up. Mostly dealers were left now, bidding against each other, nodding their heads almost imperceptibly, or tipping their cards to indicate they were still in the bidding. Cora could hardly follow them; it was all going too fast. She knew if she didn't walk up to the front of the room and ask one of Col. Bob's helpers to put the picture up, they would forget about it. Maybe Col. Bob wanted it for his wife. Maybe he had never had any intention of selling it at all.

"Twenty-nine and thirty and thirty-one! (Hasn't cost

you a cent yet!) and thirty-two. (Don't come all this way and lose it for a dollar). And thirty-three."

Cora half rose in her seat. Her dress stuck to the back of her legs. She was burning up even though she saw other people in the drafty shed pulling sweaters and jackets around themselves. She sat back down, and the old theater seat exhaled. She couldn't do it, in front of that sweet little thing sitting next to Kilby, walk up to the stage in her fat body that had never been fat with a baby and never would be now that she could read the signs everywhere for her to see.

Col. Bob leaned into the microphone now stuck in its stand. Even at the end of the evening, a smoothness about his tanned skin, cowboy hat and boots set him off from his audience. "Anyone want anything else up here?" More people were standing, some hurrying to the paying line so they wouldn't be caught waiting half the night. Cora opened her mouth. The auctioneer banged his gavel. "Auction's over. Thank you, folks."

Connor was at her side. "Let's get," he said. She broke away from him and headed for the stage where Col. Bob was helping load heavy pieces of furniture from a loading dock that opened offstage. The fever was on her, and she could feel water running down the inside of her thighs and collecting at her wrists. "That picture," she said, pointing to it with her card. "You never got to that picture." She must have looked like a crazy woman to him with her face all red like a beet, but she didn't care.

"Listen, Ma'am," Col. Bob said, grunting under the weight of a large, dark chest of drawers (genuine mahogany under the paint), "we asked if anybody wanted anything else. You shoulda' spoke up."

Cora wiped the sweat from the top of her lip with her finger. "But you didn't give me a chance. I tried to speak up, but you quit before I could."

He helped shove the chest on the bed of a pickup. His back was to her. "Ma'am, the auction's over. We didn't advertise that picture. I can't do anything about it now. You can see that."

Connor was there. She stared at him for a moment before she registered who he was.

"What's the matter with you?" he asked. "What are you doing up here?"

Cora didn't answer. It was so unfair. The night air from the open doors ate through her clothing. "Help me on with this coat," she said. "I like to get my death."

In the pickup driving home, she sat dry-eyed and saying nothing, gripping the plastic seat covers so she would not slip off.

"It's nerves," he said, over and over. "It's nerves. Them is hot spells like Mama had. It's the change and you know it. Better get some medicine for your nerves, or you're liable to go soft in the head the way your people do. Nerves, just nerves. And you doin' too much, just like I said."

"Why damn you to hell," she said, and for surprise

at her words, he almost drove the truck into a ditch. "You damned old goat. Next thing you do is tell me about how we need that girl in our house." She felt the heat start in the center of her body and radiate out to all her limbs. "Poking that thing in me all these years and never doing a bit of good with it. It ain't no change. I ain't ready for no change. There ain't nothin' happened yet!"

The bitter words, rounded and fruit-sweet to her, rasped through her throat. She knew what she wanted to say, but the words seemed to come out shredded, as though they had been forced out through a sausage grinder. The words didn't even *sound* right to her. She would never make him understand how she felt. Her eyes, tight in their sockets, popped with anger . . . no room in her head to hold it all, the opening of her mouth simply not big enough to let it out as fast as she wanted it to come. She could feel her underpants soaking, water spurting out of her like water spits from a coiled hose when the tap is first opened.

For once he had no answer for her. His eyes followed the headlights slicing through the country dark. Pulled away from him, she dozed on the vinyl seat. She dreamed of walking in blackened winter woods where leafless branches were hung with billowing scarves of silk: red, brown, and yellow . . . and with each blast of wind, the branches pierced the threads, over and over, until at last the silk was so tattered no color remained.

They All
Ran After the
Farmer's Wife

❧❧

SHE KNEW WHAT IT WAS the moment she turned
the key in the door: the awful smell, something dead,
a mouse that had bled to death somewhere, gorged on
the D-Con they had put out when they closed the
house for winter. Over her shoulder, she saw that her
husband lagged behind her as he always did when they
entered a house, a habit she had grown aware of over
the years. He sent her on ahead and unloaded luggage,
or stopped to tinker with the car, or simply stood aside—
anything to get her to encounter first whatever might
be amiss in whatever house they lived.

Tentatively to begin with, and then ignoring the
weight that settled itself near her heart, she walked
through the tiny living room, down one step to the
even tinier dining room. Though the sofa and chair,

the long handmade coffee table, the butcher's block all looked exactly as they had left them months before, the stink was tangible—an intruder lurking in a closet, prepared to take away something they prized. The crudely plastered walls had gathered up a winter's worth of cold and now threw it back at her; her breath formed little puffs as she breathed through her mouth, unwilling yet to commit herself to being there.

She heard him carry the squeaking Styrofoam cooler into the kitchen, following her, but he said nothing about the sickening odor. Was it possible he didn't notice it? Ironic that for all the yelling he did about her smoking, she ended up with the keen sense of smell. Perhaps the silence was just part of his stubbornness, or his game. She put down a bag of groceries on the sink. He was like that: don't talk to it; maybe it will go away. *Men* were like that, never wanting to discuss what really mattered.

Still there were other reasons for denying the smell. He loved the farm and was always urging her to spend more time there. She knew he didn't want the weekend off to a bad start. He might not want to call attention to what lay stinking so indelicately in a corner who knew where.

Near the refrigerator, the stink grew stronger. Actually, she thought grimly, stink was too small a word for the cloud of corruption that hung in the kitchen. She put milk, butter, and cheese away, noticed that a bottle of coke had frozen and sprayed sticky brown freckles over the jars of mustard and pickle relish they left behind in November. More mess.

Clearing his throat, he said, "I'm going out to check the electric fence." Go ahead, she thought. Leave me to deal with it. She felt like a fool peering behind the stove, sniffing, sticking her head in the bleak oven where mice like to nest in the warmth of the pilot light. Like a child's game, guessing where it was. You're getting warmer, and as the stench grew more intense, ooh, you're hot now, burning! She tried breathing through her mouth again, but didn't want to swallow the foul air as if her very lungs would be coated by the sweet stink that pervaded the house.

"Everything OK?" He brought an armload of wood into the living room, scattering chips in a trail along the secondhand oriental she had found at a yard sale.

"Yeh, yeh, everything's OK. Come in already and shut the door. It's freezing in here." The chips drove her crazy.

"It's not that cold," he said. *That* drove her crazy, too. Lately it seemed as if they existed in separate climate zones.

She wasn't going to start in though. Complain once too often, set him off, and the weekend would be ruined for certain. It depressed her, how close to the surface things still were with them. After so many years, hadn't they earned more deeply buried differences? Why did it seem sometimes that their connection was like a scarcely healed-over scab, ready to start bleeding at the smallest scrape?

Later, lying on a daybed in the living room, she read and dozed away an hour, stockinged feet to the now blazing wood stove, her shoulders toward the window where a cool March regulated her body temperature. Meanwhile, he stomped in and out, unloading the rest of the car, carrying in more wood, turning on the water. Each time he opened the door, an icy draft preceded him and followed in his wake. She clenched her teeth, said nothing.

"So, is that it for you for the day?" he asked finally, looking down at her.

He looks ridiculous, she thought, in a heavy sweater, down vest, denim jacket, and a French beret he had rescued from some bag bound for the thrift shop. Slowly she lowered the book to her chest. "And what if it is? I've worked like a dog all week. I have a right to lie around on my ass if I want to."

He threw a log into the stove and clanged the door shut with his foot. "Well. I'm going to take a walk," he said, self-righteously. "You can waste the day if you want to."

"Have a good time," she said, and then under her breath, "Quit trying to run my life!" After awhile, the book took hold again, and she floated away: spies, nukes, Moscow and London, another kind of corruption. From time to time, she was aware of the stench spilling out of the kitchen, coming between her and the story. What a nuisance. She ought to get at the source, get rid of it before he came back. A good wife would do that. He loved the place so. She could do that for him, and she would . . . later.

She dreamed of George Raft, Jimmy Cagney, Edward G. Robinson, pugnacious little men in fedoras circling the farmhouse with submachine guns. "You little rat," they muttered in chorus, "you little rat!" "They all ran after the farmer's wife," sang George Raft. His black hair shone like patent leather tap shoes. Edward G. Robinson took the chewed stub of a cigar from his mouth and looked at it, smiling evilly; his face was as wrinkled as the cross section of a cabbage. He sang in a piping falsetto, "She cut off their tails with a carving knife." Brandishing the machine gun, Jimmy Cagney growled, "I smell a rat." Had someone ratted on a friend? What was the crime? Something hidden deep that couldn't be masked by cover-ups.

When she awoke, her husband was lying outstretched on the other sofa across the room from her. The smell was stronger, intensified perhaps by the warmth of the stove. "I don't know if I can stay here with that terrible odor," he said, mentioning it at last. He's embarrassed by it, she thought. Stinks are embarrassing. He uses the word "odor" to put it more delicately. She felt sorry for him then. She knew he had a picture in his mind of how the weekend would unfurl, and now everything was twisted and wrong. It would have been so easy, but she couldn't bring herself to say the soothing words. "You have the right things to say to everyone but me." He was always telling her that. Maybe it was true. Still the moment passed, and she lay silent.

He said, "Maybe we should go into town for dinner. How can you cook in that?" Hearing no answer, he got up and opened the front door and those at either end of the kitchen. Then he lay down on the couch, this time turning his back to her. At the rear of the house, a cold wind blew through what was now a tunnel. She could hear the rattle of the newspapers she had put down to sop up water that leaked when he had turned on the pump. Go ahead; turn your back on it, she thought. Why do I always have to deal with the shit? I hate this place: dead flies speckling the window sills and worse. She drew in her shoulders as another wasp flew out of nowhere and batted the wall behind her.

The room grew colder; she shivered and wrapped herself in a multicolored afghan. Outside the land provided too many open spaces. She needed corners to cozy into; one side exposed was danger enough. She got dizzy out there, unable to find a spot where brambles didn't reach out to snag her sweater or her pants.

He was different. He rambled all over the land, walked miles of fences, stood for hours on the banks of the pond they had dug, stared into the water and needed no fish for excuse. But then, he was a runner and thought nothing of walking out the door in the city in skimpy shorts and sleeveless shirt to jog for miles. So many years of running, and if he fell on the path one day and needed her, she wouldn't know the route he took or where to find him though he'd told her a thousand times. He's right, she thought. I don't listen to what he says half the time.

They were two hours from home. She knew he would never agree simply to pack up again and turn back. In the end he was stubborn and would want to get to the root of the stench, unlike her who would have shut the doors and left the dead thing to dry up and disappear. The fact was they had both looked forward to a weekend in the country, although with the kids grown and gone, the house in town was quiet enough. The farm was a change, at least, and now the stink was driving them out.

He rolled over onto his back and stared up at the ceiling where a wasp crawled slowly in and out of a ceiling fixture. "Just don't bother it," he said. "They won't sting you if you just leave them alone."

"Who's bothering it?" she replied, accepting the admonition as an opening peace maneuver. "I've got troubles enough already."

Encouraged by her tone, his voice grew louder as if the volume of their combined voices might be sufficient to take the house back again. "Randy's cattle have gotten into the pond again. We've got to call him and find out if he's willing to fix the fence. Otherwise, let him rent from someone else this year. Are you hearing me?" he asked sharply.

"I'm hearing you," she said.

He went on. "The trouble is, we never call him. We say we will but we don't."

"What do you mean 'we,' White Man?" Their old joke came easily. Domestic shorthand.

He pulled himself to a sitting position, then swung his legs onto the floor. "You think that's funny, but if I don't call him nobody will. You never make those phone calls."

"So I'll call him, and I won't be sure what to ask, and you'll have plenty to say about it later. You want me to make the call, but then you're never satisfied with what I say."

"You know me," he said, ignoring the jab. "I can't understand half of what they're talking about out here. I'm a city boy, remember?"

"I know, I know," she said, feeling guilty, wondering what he would do if she admitted how many times she made phone calls in the country and put her finger down on the receiver so she could say no one was at home. She *did* leave that kind of thing to him . . . a way of covering herself if there were a misunderstanding, and there usually was.

"Where's the magazine section of the *Times?*" he asked, abruptly changing the subject.

She thought, Oh, God, here we go. "I didn't touch it," she said, too quickly.

"Well, I don't see it." He fumbled through the pile of papers on the coffee table in front of him. "You've probably been cleaning again. I put something down for five minutes, and you're all over it. Two houses and I haven't any place for myself. Why don't you worry about your own mess, and just leave me my few square feet?"

She threw off the afghan, sat up, and turned to face him. "Are you going to start that shit again? You get me out here, and you know I have nowhere to go. I'm trapped. Then you start picking on me. It's freezing in here. I want to go home!" She slammed the front door and stood warming her back at the wood stove. Despite the airing, the smell of decay was stronger than ever.

What in the world was this all about? The ride down had been pleasant enough, each of them slowly letting go of the previous week, companionably marking off the milestones as city and suburbs fell away, and the country finally took over. But she was into it now, carried along on the argument's tide like a twig or a matchstick. Unaccountably, each quarrel felt original, as if they had never fought or made up in the past. Panicked, she seemed to lose all memory of how she had saved herself the time before.

Just be quiet, she said to herself. Just don't say anymore; but she couldn't be still. "You carry on about my cleaning, but the one time in ten years you come home and find the coffeepot left from breakfast, I hear about it."

"I was surprised," he said, defensively. "You never do that. I meant it as a compliment."

She wanted a cigarette badly, but decided she wasn't up for that kind of escalation. "What you're saying is I can't win. Clean, don't clean; which way do you want it? What do you want from me?" The question hung in the air like smoke, its implications spreading as it dissipated.

"Why don't you try to be quiet for awhile?" he said. "Forget it."

"Forget it; forget it," she mocked. "Sure, you start in, and then when I try to defend myself, you tell me to be quiet. You get it off your chest, and I'm supposed to swallow it. That's having it both ways, isn't it?"

He tucked his hands into the pockets of his down vest and didn't answer. Now he was going into his disappearing act. Now she would really be alone. His briefcase stood open on the floor next to the sofa where he sat. She reached over and snatched the magazine from its yawning mouth. "Here's your goddamn *Times*, right where you put it." She flung it at him. "I told you I didn't touch your fucking paper!" He held his hand up and made a sign to her, a duck's beak, opening and closing.

"Ayy," she said, clicking her tongue, knowing the argument was over, the air cleared, that she was in grace again, remembering how it was with them. "You make me sick," she said, without conviction.

She risked a cigarette then, certain that in the spirit of détente he would say nothing. All afternoon she had been waiting for the Nat Cole lecture. Every public figure who died of lung cancer provided an object lesson, but as he told her over and over, "It doesn't seem to stop you." What did almost stop her was his confession one evening that he had nightmares about her dying. "I don't know if I would want to live without you," he had said, simply.

"Well," she said, stubbing out the cigarette, "here goes nothing."

"Where are you going?"

"To see if that's an arm Hansel is sticking out of the cage, or only a chicken bone."

"You're nuts,' he said. "I don't know what you are talking about."

In the kitchen she shoved a broom handle behind the stove and pulled the stick along the floor. Nothing dislodged but gray balls of dust. The cloying smell threatened to overwhelm her sense of purpose. She felt betrayed somehow that something once alive should inspire in her such revulsion. There had been too much studiedly casual talk, lately, of too many empty bedrooms in their house in town, of slowing down, retirement. She felt as young as ever, but memory and the calendar fought her with a state-of-the-art arsenal. In self-defense she was reduced to reading the inside of matchbook covers for the seven danger signs of this or that, and always a symptom evoked an answering twinge, and she was afraid.

Now she sniffed at the burners again, but the stove wasn't the source. And she couldn't find anything when she pushed the refrigerator away from the wall or when she hung over the sink to peer down between it and the pump. Still she thought, I'm burning, burning.

"Listen," she called. "Is there a way to get into the water heater? I think that's your problem." She moved back while he took a screwdriver and unscrewed the white enamel front panel of the water heater where it stood in line with the sink and refrigerator.

"I don't know about this," he said, clearly apprehensive. "Maybe we should give up and call someone, a cleaning service or something."

"It's our problem; let's deal with it."

Yellowed cotton batting protected and insulated the heater's wires—a tangle of Medusa locks. The stink was powerful now, and she could see torn bits of paper she recognized as signs of a nest. "Here it is," she told him, gingerly grabbing a piece of paper that came away in her hands along with droppings the size of raisins.

She fell silent, wishing she could shield him from her suspicions. Wasn't that marriage, too? You revealed things you'd never tell another soul, but in the end what you held back was a greater gift. Wasn't holding back what you finally did for one another? This was no ordinary mouse.

She pulled at a corner of blue material and yanked out a paper dishcloth speckled with more droppings, then a pink cloth napkin, more paper, plastic bags so chewed they were barely recognizable. "I'm getting sick," she told him. He stood near a door open to the outside as if prepared to run at any moment.

"You know me," he said. "I'm a city boy."

She giggled nervously and then began to cry. "I can't do this. I don't care anymore. I'm not going to reach in there again." Backing up to the range, she wiped her nose with the back of her hand, sniffing.

"I don't blame you," he said. "Maybe we shouldn't have started in, but we've got to finish now. Maybe a stick and some gloves . . ."

She stepped close to the water heater again. "Jesus, I think I see its tail. Gimme the gloves!" With the yardstick, she made a pass at the coiled black thing behind the batting. She couldn't dislodge it. The "tail" was a wrapped electrical wire, and still she plucked paper, plastic, and cloth from the opening, "It's your turn," she told him, gorge rising. "You do it if you're so brave."

"I'm not brave," he said taking the gloves from her.

Though she turned her back, she couldn't leave the room. Something in her had to discover what had taken over the house in their absence.

"I think I've got it," he said, his voice too loud for the tiny kitchen. Reaching into the cotton one last time, he snatched the flattened dead rat from its hiding place and dropped it on the floor as if it were a live wire. The stiffened body hit the linoleum with a thud she felt through the soles of her feet and at the back of her tensed calves. Dead weight, she said to herself. Now I know what that means.

With a broom and dustpan, she scooped it up, crossed the kitchen, and flung the dead thing far to the side of the porch where some nighttime predator would soon pick it down to a harmless heap of bones. But that wasn't the end of it. She knew she would be a long time forgetting the image of the brown rat like some perversion of a precious jewel, resting so neatly in its bed of cotton.

Presents

THE GAME IS FIENDISH. While she stands fiddling with the microphone, a hundred pairs of eyes ranging from studiedly indifferent to downright hostile give her the covert once-over. Her short breaths, dragged through stuffy sinuses and picked up by the mike, ride the crest of our clamor and crackle to the corners of Lachman's Kosher Katering. Waitresses in black uniforms with ruffly white aprons have cleared the round tables at which we sit of everything but coffee cups and ashtrays. Now they swing by one last time, nonchalantly endangering lives, pouring streams of boiling coffee from aluminum pitchers.

She says, "Testing, one, two, three," then shrugs and puts her palms out helplessly. "Can you hear me?" her amplified voice asks. I'm relieved to turn toward the head table, away from the empty parfait glass whose depths I have plumbed with a long-handled spoon, again and again, until the tip is brassy on my tongue, away from the grown-up conversation that taxes me as if it were a foreign language I am just now learning how to speak.

In moments I realize that just as I do not yet know their language, so am I unfamiliar with their customs, for I've done it again; I am the only one who has shifted position; nobody else has budged. Around me, women sip their coffee and clatter their cups in their saucers; they puff their Chesterfields and Camels and Pall Malls. "Can you hear me?" she says again, but the hubbub continues as if she hadn't spoken.

Thrown to the lions in this social arena, I find myself as outwardly defenseless as the Christian martyrs of old. For one thing, I haven't mastered the killer wedge implicit in, "My son, the doctor," or "my car, the Cadillac." Not like my luncheon partner who has introduced herself as Mimi; she is one of those women who seems to have been born knowing the rules. Among other things, she didn't flick an eyelash at the mike's beseeching, while I have already marked myself a greenhorn as surely as if I had walked in here wearing a babushka and carrying my comb and wallet in a bundle instead of a purse.

During dessert Mimi held the entire table in thrall, regaling us with how she coped when her furnace went out during last week's blizzard. "It's a brand new furnace," she assured us, "still on the warranty. We just moved into our ranch on Northfield Boulevard and we don't even have the *pool* in yet, but I call the builder and, believe you me, I let him have it. He promises he'll get a man on it right away. In the meantime, the laundress is complaining she's freezing so I let her take the other Cadillac and go home for a while, but I can't leave because it's the maid's day off, and I'm the only one left to wait for the repairman."

By this time, she has everyone's rapt attention, and she gives it everything she's got, and trust me, to hear her tell it, that's plenty. "The house gets colder by the minute, and I'm worried that the pipes are going to freeze," she goes on. "Can you imagine the mess with four bedrooms and the family room and two-and-a-half baths? And wouldn't you know it, the nurse tells me my husband's with a patient so he's no help. Finally, I just go upstairs and get under the chintz spread I had made at Hudson's and I'm still cold so I have to get up and wrap myself in my full-length mink."

Now it's pretty clear that if one-upmanship is a parachute to survival here, I'm the kid without a rip cord. Not to take all this personally, of course, but who doesn't, and by my count, she put me down approximately ten times in that "I-me-mine" monologue. We're a long way from Northfield Boulevard, David and I, if that's where we're heading; right now the best we can do is the sun porch at his mother's and a space heater.

What always puzzles me about such group schmoozing is the conversational underbelly that's conveniently forgotten: the bent twig of a disappointing child, the plodding business that gives salt sweat for return, the rank sheets of a marriage gone sour. In the presence of such silence, I find no communicational toehold; my feet go scrambling for purchase in negative space.

So ask me what I'm doing here? I never would have come in the first place if the bride's mother hadn't attended my shower. That's the kind of social black-mail that keeps Lachman in Chryslers. All these women do for kicks is go to each others' affairs. My mother would certainly have put in an appearance if she were alive. She and the bride's mother were girlfriends in the Old Country. So for my mother, maybe, I put on the one outfit that still goes round my middle, and here I sit wondering if my gift will make it though the gauntlet of those assessing eyes.

You could call this a rather modest event as these things go; Lachman can accommodate two-hundred and fifty people when he removes the fake-Chinese room-divider screens, and for some reason today he has, so we are made small in a space that could handle the University of Michigan marching band. There's Snow White at the mike and almost a gross of post-prandial dwarfs in attendance, all of them, if I am an example, named "Sleepy." The chartreuse walls that surround us are cut in half by a Greek key design stenciled at eye level, probably more to bring the ceilings down a little than for any attempt at beautifying the place. Lachman's decorator should be condemned to live here.

At last, my Aunt Dora, one of the hostesses, places a practiced hand over the microphone and whispers in Snow White's ear. The PA system emits a retaliatory whine, and I can feel Lachman's fish coming up on me. Why did I eat so much? I'm too fat to live, but given the chance, I got caught up in the combative atmosphere and risked a puncture wound from the other flailing forks all stabbing madly away at the platter of *Lokshen kugel*.

"Ladies," Aunt Dora is saying, "may I have your attention, *please*." You can tell she has rank in this group for now the shushing begins, rising like steam from a radiator, first from one table and then another. And, as if she has further signaled them, another kind of brouhaha ensues. With a great scraping, the women, some still puffing their cigarettes, dragging their chairs in their wake, elbow their way to the head table. My Aunt Frieda motions to an empty seat she has pulled up almost directly opposite the bride-to-be. "I saved you a place," she says. Aunt Frieda is one of those still centers in hurricanes' eyes. Who else would have ended up front row, center, in such a melee?

In front of us, a young girl of twelve or so snips the bow on a large package with a pair of beribboned shears, her pinched face a miniature of Snow White's.

Expertly she tears off the wrapping, tucks the top of the box under the bottom, and shoves it all down the table. By the time she's old enough for her turn at the mike, she'll be doing this in her sleep.

"From Mrs. Morris Aronowitz," says the bride, squinting at the card, "a lovely set of Cannon towels." It's obvious from the way she stares blankly out at us that she doesn't know Mrs. Aronowitz from Adam, and I don't notice anyone rushing to help her either. She waves the pink towels limply like a feeble SOS. "Where are you, Mrs. Aronowitz?" she asks.

From somewhere behind me, a voice replies grudgingly, "Here I am."

"Thank you, Mrs. Aronowitz," says the bride, and the showing of the presents has begun.

I have opened the last set of snaps on my expandable skirt, and pretending I am anything but what I am, a nineteen-year-old woman ready to deliver, is an exercise in futility. As if I didn't feel put down enough in this collective fashion show, my entire maternity wardrobe consists of a brown print rayon dress my cousin Bernice gave me, a black-and-white hound's-tooth jumper, and the scabrous corduroy suit I have on now. When I finally get to the hospital, if I live that long, David has strict orders to burn all three outfits because I never want to see them again, not even on some other poor sucker.

"And from Mrs. Milton Friedberg, a G.E. clock radio," says the bride. "For our *bedroom*," she adds coyly.

She's into it now and getting creative. There are titters from the women and an appreciative ripple of applause as she holds up a cream-colored bakelite case.

"Mrs. Friedberg," calls the bride, "where are you?"

"She had to leave early. She had another affair," someone finally announces.

"Well, thank you anyway, Mrs. Friedberg," says Snow White, lamely.

Looming up out of nowhere, the groom's mother grabs the microphone from her future daughter-in-law. "She better not depend on that radio to get *Morty* up in the morning," she tells the crowd. Rattled, the bride reaches for the next enclosure card, but her voice is drowned out in derisive laughter.

"How do you like that outfit?" asks Aunt Frieda, nodding in the bride's direction. "It's the 'new look,' " I tell her. "The fashion magazines are full of it." "New, schmew," says my aunt as she casually smooths the hem of her print dress where it ends just below her knees. "The girl looks like an old *bobbe* in that long skirt." "Well," I say, finding the correct response at last, "it certainly is different."

I recognize the "new look" from the fashion magazines I've taken to reading at the doctor's. Convince me there isn't something sadistic about an O.B. who furnishes his office with pictures of models so skinny they can't eat an apple without it showing the way a mouse does when a snake swallows it whole. It's a mine field out there, Snow White, and your Baby Louis heels will never pass for ruby slippers.

It's not easy being a woman, and we don't help each other much. Still, whatever else marriage does, it takes some of the pressure off. I haven't forgotten those wrestling matches in the backseats of cars, or waking up the morning after like someone out of *The Penal Colony* with the pattern of the living room carpet tattooed on my tush . . . and what about studying the calendar each month as if it were Talmud? Maybe Snow White doesn't worry. Maybe she's a virgin still with that prissy face. But if she isn't, I'll bet she's holding her breath until her boyfriend smashes that wineglass.

Behind the head table, Aunt Dora is doing a shimmy, holding up in front of her a filmy nightgown someone has given the bride. Encased in her corset, Aunt Dora looks for all the world like an animated stuffed *kishka*. The women are hooting and clapping their hands. Snow White is as red as a beet. She *must* be a virgin.

"That Dora: she's such a comedian," my aunt Frieda says, but I can tell she would like to take her sister-in-law out to Belle Isle and drown her. I just wish they would open my gift and get it over with. By this time, I know it's a stupid present.

Over in a corner near the exit, a handful of men are causing a small commotion. You can spot the groom by his slightly droopy carnation and the white satin yarmulke on the crisp, brown curls at the crown of his head. A couple of older guys, probably his father and the father of the bride, flank him, hands in their

pockets. They look about as out of place here as deb-
utantes at a *mikva*. I recognize the husband-to-be; he
and I were in the same study hall at Central. He was
one of those young men born to star in women's dreams,
with eyes the color of meadow larks and long arms
meant for draping over the leather seatbacks of con-
vertibles or around the narrow shoulders of a girl . . .

For warm-ups in junior-high drama class, we used
to do pronunciation exercises. One of them was, "Do
not seek to join the clique." Over and over I practiced
it: "Do not seek to join the clique." The sentence sang
in my head, a leitmotif, and all the while I spent my
waking hours (and sleeping ones, too, probably), trying
to figure out how to do just the opposite.

We moved to Detroit the year I entered eighth grade.
On the first day of school, I picked out someone for
my best friend. I wasn't stupid; I didn't set my sights
on any of the obviously "popular" girls, the ones who
held their schoolbooks at a heartbreaking angle, casually revealing pastel cashmeres draped over bras shaped
like the nose cones of B-29s. I stayed away from the
clusters of boys and girls, giggling and posturing, at
home with one another, and—even more intimidating
to me—so at home with themselves.

Instead, I moved in on a dumpy red-head with glasses
who answered my tentative smile with one of her own.
I learned later that smile had earned her the title of
most popular girl in the class. She bestowed it with
about as much discrimination as it takes to flip a light

switch. No, she couldn't eat lunch in the cafeteria with me that day, and she was booked for the rest of the week, too. I didn't seek to join the clique much after that. Seeing Snow White up there and her groom brings it all back somehow.

Which doesn't mean I don't feel sorry for her in a way, standing on the platform, decked out for judging like a prize heifer at the state fair. Women don't give one another much slack. I remember sitting nervously at the edge of a chair in a crowded waiting room not long ago. Around me a dozen other women of varying ages chatted or flipped through magazines. The women with the swelling bellies were easy to place, but the one sitting next to me, glossy as a cricket, her stomach so flat it curved inward: Was she here for the same reason I was?

"I know you," the woman said suddenly, turning to me. "I'm Laurie Weiss, your cousin Bernice's friend. Her mother just threw you a shower; am I right?"

A nurse opened one of the office's inner doors and said, "Beth, will you come in, please?"

Across from where Laurie and I sat, a very pregnant woman pushed herself out of her chair and disappeared behind the door. Laurie twisted her engagement ring so I would be sure to see it, an emerald-cut rock the size of a matzo ball. "This is your first internal; am I right?"

Yes, she was right, and I had a vision of the doctor reaching with gloved hand clear up through my body until his fingers waved out of my mouth like a cluster of extra tongues.

"You'll love it," Laurie said.

My package with its unmistakable shape is just hitting the end of the assembly line. Little Sister has done such an efficient job she is taking a break to work on the ribbon bouquet, pushing streamers through a small box-top. The bride is holding up a couple of white towels between her thumb and forefinger. Though her face is as blank as a china plate, her other three fingers form a rooster's comb of distaste.

The woman-noise around me begins to rise and fall like the thrumming of insects on an autumn afternoon. Aunt Dora, arms crossed on her bosom, looks as if Uncle Al has just invited her to have sex on the hood of their Chrysler New Yorker. "What's going on?" I ask Aunt Frieda. I'm stung suddenly at how old she looks. Her pretty wax-doll features are drooping as though they'd been left out in the sun too long.

"It's the *meshugeneh*," she tells me, "Lotte Brenner," as if that explains everything; but I still don't understand. "Those towels are from the business," Aunt Frieda says. "So?" My aunt is impatient or embarrassed; I don't know which, and I'm probably digging my greenhorn grave a little deeper, but I persist. "Her husband runs a linen supply, and whenever she has to give a gift, she brings used towels. I don't know who she thinks she's fooling," says my aunt. "It's a crying shame."

The story of Mrs. Brenner comes back to me, now that I'm reminded. Over the years, I've heard the women gossip about it and the men laugh, but evidently Mrs. Brenner just keeps on doing it. She won't get out of the game, but she makes a mockery of the rules. Aunt Frieda calls her crazy, and Aunt Dora says she's just plain cheap. I think what really unsettles them all is her *chutzpa*—there she sits in that roomfull of accusing fingers stonily confident that she won't get her eyes poked out.

"Where are you, Mrs. Brenner?" asked Snow White, looking down at the table.

"Don't try to take *those* back to Hudson's," mutters Aunt Frieda.

"Obviously, she's a first class cheap-skate," I tell my aunt, grown-up-woman-talk, but almost immediately feel as if I have somehow betrayed Mrs. Brenner in my eagerness to edge over to the other side of the line. I can't shake off the guilt. How should I know why she does what she does? Long ago I learned how easily soft assumptions harden into givens. I think of all the women who are dear to me and wonder why we are so quick to eat each other's bones. Haven't I seen one woman crucify another for a fallen cake or a Monday line of dingy wash?

The afternoon settles on my shoulders with intolerable weight. "Let me out, Aunt Frieda," I say. "I have to go to the ladies'." A couple of my mother's friends give me long, sad looks as I squeeze past their knees. "Poor thing," one of them says. I don't know whether she means me or my mother.

Lachman's bathroom is the same chartreuse as the dining room. Left-over paint, I suppose. In any event, all that yellowish-green makes me feel like I'm inside gallons of raw chicken liver. To add to my misery, all three stalls are occupied. My cousin Sadie is waiting, too, ensconced in front of a mirror, wiping lipstick from her teeth with a bit of toilet paper.

"Sit down, Honey," she says. "You look tired."

Sadie always tells people they look tired. The result is they feel lousy after she's greeted them no matter how well they felt before.

A toilet flushes, and a small woman emerges from one of the cubicles. She spots me standing in line.

"It's your next," she says. "The rest of them can wait."

Stupidly I hesitate for a moment while she holds open the stall door.

"Go on," she says, giving me a gentle push on the shoulder. "They know how it is."

I realize it's Mrs. Brenner and blushing, I disappear into the booth, too embarrassed even to thank her and certain she overheard me call her cheap.

The little room is still crowded when I get out of the stall. Sadie is waiting for me. "You look nice, Sadie," I tell her, not knowing what else to say. Sadie has inherited the Wollenberg nose, a formidable legacy. People call her "peppy." She puts on a brave show: glittering glass rings and brooches, necklaces, and earrings. A rhinestone-studded watch blazes on her lapel, and an equally brilliant watch vies for attention among the many bracelets on her plump wrist.

"Thanks, Honey," she says, preening in the mirror. "I was worried this ring might be a little too much."

I haven't the energy to rush out and claim credit for my shower present just yet, so I lean against the chartreuse wall watching Sadie comb her hair. At home in the front closet, my bag is packed, ready to go: brand-new night gown still in its tissue, new slippers, a toothbrush and toothpaste, a hairbrush and comb. Anticipation and apprehension have been duking it out inside me for weeks.

"Someone's talking to you," says Sadie.

"Pardon?"

"I was just remarking to the girls, you look like you were due yesterday."

The blue-haired lady with the potato-grater voice wears a circle of fox furs around her neck, each one biting the tail of the next. If there is a proper response to her observation, it doesn't spring to my lips.

"You'll have a boy," she continues, apparently undaunted by my silence. "Look at her!" she says loudly, leaning forward to pat my jutting belly. "You see that *spitz?* Turn around!" she commands, and I'm too stunned to do anything but obey. "What did I tell you? She's carrying all in the front. It's a boy!"

"*Bobbe-mysehs*" says Mrs. Brenner from the sinks opposite us where she is drying her hands. "It's all fifty-fifty, anyway."

"And who asked you your opinion?" says the fox fur, haughtily.

Mrs. Brenner crumples the paper towel and tosses it in a wastebasket. "The same person who asked you yours," she says.

The air in Lachman's Ladies' Lounge is getting decidedly frosty, but just as I turn to make my getaway, Sadie's sister, Merle, walks in.

"Grand Central Station," she says, looking around and cracking her gum. Too bad we're not men. Looks like we've got enough for a *minyan* in here."

With her great masses of black hair, Merle always reminds me of the girl in the do-you-want-longer-hair? ads. She has shaved her eyebrows and penciled in little mouse holes so she looks perpetually surprised, although she is a woman whom nothing surprises. Evidently my condition fills her with instant nostalgia, for she and Sadie immediately begin trading war stories about their deliveries.

"What about you?" Merle says, finally turning to me. "Any false labor yet?"

"Not yet, Merle," I say, dropping my guard for a moment. Actually, I've been thinking about that a lot. What if I'm one of those who can't tell false labor from real? What if I wait until the last minute, and the car won't start? Very casually I say, "To tell the

truth, Merle, I'm a little worried I won't know the difference."

Merle looks surprised, though I remind myself she's not.

"You'll know, believe me." She raises the mouse-holes and says dramatically, "My first real labor pain threw me clear across the room!"

Now everybody wants to get into the act, and the only neutral corner seems to be an empty toilet stall. I walk in and lock the door, not certain of what to do. Voices battle it out for who had the most stitches and the longest labor. Spinal, caudal, Demerol, sodium pentothal: the words click aginst each other coldly like instruments in a metal basin.

To hell with anyone who has to go. I'll stay in here until they all leave. It's too late to be afraid of having a baby, even though I am. Why don't they shut up? I can hear Fox Fur adding her two cents worth about blue babies and strangling on cords. How am I going to get out of here?

Last night I dreamed about when my brother was born at home. In the dream, my mother's sister came to wake me. "You must stay in bed today," she said. "Mama needs you to be a good girl. The new baby is coming." All day the snow fell outside my window, softly filling up the world until I thought it might somehow sift in through the chimney and begin to pile upon the carpets . . . But what are those sounds I have never heard before, tearing great holes in the silence? Soon the snow will reach my bed feet and her bed too, slowly drifting blanket upon blanket until my face is covered and my ears and the sound my crying makes and that scarlet cry from her room, all quieted soon under cushions of cold . . . When I awoke, I felt the baby stir under my heart, and I could not brush off the dream that clung like cobwebs.

"Are you OK in there?"

Someone is knocking on the stall door. "I'm fine, I'm fine," I say, brushing past Sadie and Merle and the woman in the fox furs. "I just need some fresh air."

It is Mrs. Brenner who holds the outside door open for me. For a moment, I imagine she has stayed behind to protect me from the others. She is a coiled wire of a woman, as nondescript as a sparrow.

"Tell them all to kiss your ass," she says, looking intently at me, her eyes suddenly brimming.

We stand for a moment at the threshold of the dining room where tall electric fans recirculate stale cigarette smoke and the greasy aftermath of long-ago devoured fish. Mrs. Brenner rests a hand on my shoulder, a weightless and insistent little bird claw.

"Who listens to them?" she says in Yiddish. "You'll go like everybody goes, when the time is right, and your mother, may she rest in peace, will look out for you."

A few guests are already starting to leave; some carry arrangements of yellow mums that were the centerpieces for each round table. At my side, the little woman gives off a dusty energy, and I'm fearful some of her strangeness will transmit itself to me. Her eccentricity unnerves me; it's centrality I'm seeking while she seems to be willing me outside the circle. I don't know the story of her otherness, but her ability to slough off judgments makes me uneasy. I want to be integral to the design, not the lonely afterthought of fringe.

Showers, weddings, monthly blood, and births: the bride and I are taking part in a grand initiation. All of us go through it. Even Snow White's little sister is already pledged. How we perform or conform simply measures our fitness to belong. What went on in the doctor's waiting room and in the ladies' room was a kind of hazing; I ought to know that by now.

So I'm not completely part of these other women yet. Sometimes I wonder if I ever will be. Still, I haven't the courage to be an outcast . . . cast out like a pair of dice with only chance to add up my numbers. If I pull myself away as Mrs. Brenner has, who will drop crumbs along the path for me? What blazes will I follow? I ask this, and yet, deep down I know there must be a way to make difference a positive force— to add complexity to the design rather than unbalance it.

"Maybe I better get back inside," I tell Mrs. Brenner, anxious to free myself from the burden of that small dry claw. I leave her there in the doorway, but

I can feel the touch on my shoulder all the way back to my seat.

"I was worried about you," Aunt Frieda says. "You missed your present." She looks at me curiously. "Well," she says, keeping an eye on Snow White who is holding up a place setting of her "everyday" china, "it certainly was different. A couple of the girls had to ask what it was."

I close my eyes as Aunt Frieda pinches my cheek.

"Honey, she says, "what are we going to do with you?"

In Going
Is a Drama

IN THE MIDDLE OF THE QUARREL, Sorrel dropped
to the floor, but not before she caught the look on
Joseph's face. He would have drowned her in a tea-
spoon of water if that feat were only possible. She lay
prone, breathing the acrid dirt trapped in the woven
flowers.

Sorrel could hear Tova jumping from place to place.
Tova yelled, "Mama, please stop that! Mama, get up!"
Yet Joseph said nothing. He couldn't wait to get rid
of her. Sorrel felt that. And the girl: her tears were
false. She always took her father's side, and she would
be happy soon enough with her mother out of the
way . . . she and that Rasputin together. Well, let her
see if a stepmother would treat her any better than her
own mother did. Poor Tova.

Sorrel tried to hold her body still. Only minutes

ago, the lines of the argument had seemed so clearly drawn. Now she couldn't for the life of her remember what it had been about. No matter; she pitied the girl, although no one appeared to pity *her*. If only Joseph would reach out a hand to touch her, but he stood there silent and stolid as a butcher's block. Tova whined, "Daddy, do something. Maybe she's dead. Oh, please."

"I don't know what she wants from me," Joseph said. "You see how she carries on."

Tova knelt near Sorrel's face and put her own face so close that Sorrel could feel the warm breath bubbling through the girl's nostrils as she sobbed. There was a limit to what Sorrel could do to her own flesh and blood. She opened her eyes, looked straight into her daughter's eyes for a moment, then gave an exaggerated wink. Tova jumped back, confused.

The child's sobbing slowed to hiccups. Sorrel could feel the floorboards move under her face as Joseph walked away. Where was he going now? Nothing would melt him. Then the floor boards creaked once more. He stood over her. She could see the shining black tips of his good shoes, smell the fresh polish. Would he touch her now, tell her the quarrel was foolish, admit it was his fault?

Tova screamed, "Daddy!"

Sorrel started as the cold water ran down the back of her head and neck and dripped onto the carpet. The bastard! She turned over and moaned, one hand flung over her face.

"Will you stop eating my bones?" Joseph said. He

handed Tova the empty pitcher and reached for one of Sorrel's arms. Encircling her waist, he lifted her and walked her to an armchair.

"Tova," he said to the red-eyed girl, "you are late for school."

She hesitated, looking at her mother who sat, hair matted, staring blankly at the stippled plaster walls.

"She'll be all right. Marta's coming." Joseph opened his fists, then clenched them again.

Sniffling, Tova picked up her schoolbooks from an end table near the sofa and left the room.

"Doesn't the girl have enough already without this?" Joseph asked gently enough. "Please, Sorrel, I'm late opening the store."

"So go already," she replied. "Who needs you here?"

Joseph tried once more. "How can you get better this way?" He turned as if he did not expect an answer, and said, "Calm yourself."

"Calm yourself," she mocked bitterly, but he had already left the room.

Moments later, she heard the front door slam. Cut glass prisms, hanging from a floor lamp's wrought-iron leaves, tinkled in response. Sorrel swallowed green gall. "Calm yourself," she repeated. She wished she had hit him hard, had pounded him with the back of her fists so the false words might have come flying out like a half-chewed piece of meat lodged in the wrong place. She said no more. No point in talking to walls, but she felt strength pour out of her like sugar from a torn sack.

Bit by bit, the morning began to come back to her. She was certain she hadn't been the cause of the argument this time. They had been quietly eating breakfast, and she recalled now, it was something about his hair, combed straight back from his forehead the way it always was that started it. She had watched him run his palm over it as he read the paper, saw him caress the fine black hair almost as a woman might do to him. And the words popped out, innocently enough, she thought. "Rosie staying late with you for stock taking?"

He had knocked over a water glass in his anger. "Are you starting in already?"

Tova leapt up and mopped the table with a dish towel, always eager to get on his good side.

"For God's sake," he continued, "aren't you ashamed in front of the child?"

At the memory of his rebuke, Sorrel's cheeks burned again like the red-hot filament of a radio tube which glows briefly after the power has been turned off. She wasn't making it up. There *was* something between Joseph and that woman, and it was killing her.

"It's killing me," Sorrel said aloud, combing her heavy brown hair with her fingers. She longed to go back to bed a little while, but that seemed so irresponsible. All the other women in the neighborhood, she knew, would be finishing their second cups of coffee, stripping beds, vacuuming their floors. Only Marta saw how much time she had to spend in bed.

Still, it would be good to put her head down, just

for a moment, there on the davenport; she wouldn't get in bed so it hardly counted. She needed the rest. The doctor had told her to take it easy . . . so she would get well. Fear washed over her then, turned her bowels to water; she had to sit down and hug herself. And what difference would it really make? One day soon they would pull the covers over her head, and she would not get up again. She wandered aimlessly around the room, emptied butts from the smoking stand into a paper bag, straightened the edge of the carpet where Tova had kicked it, and then gave in and lay down on the sofa.

In the dream she poked her finger in her nose and tore at the tender flesh at the base of her nostril. Under her fingernail, something rounded and slimy gathered itself. With thumb and forefinger she grasped the substance and began to pull. Slowly she drew a long worm from her nose, leaving a snail track on her upper lip, and then, when the worm snapped off like a rubber band, she clawed again and pulled again, an endless worm that looped and coiled itself around her.

It seemed she thrashed and flailed for many moments before she became aware that her cousin, Asnah, stood before her. Though Sorrel had not seen her for many years, she did not think it strange that Asnah wore the same dark dress and heavy woolen shawl in which she'd run for almost a mile alongside the wagon that carried Sorrel and her family to the train that started them on their journey out of Poland.

Sorrel snapped her fingers backward, but the worm, clinging stubbornly, refused to part from her hand. Desperately, she snapped her fingers again, for Asnah would not want to see it, would be disgusted by the sickening thing. Now she was certain her cousin would pass her by, and she would lose track of her, for good this time. She snapped her fingers once more, and the worm fell writhing into a clot on the floor.

Sorrel ran to Asnah and embraced her, but she was shocked at the feel of her . . . like a paper bag blown up with air or a pillow lightly stuffed with eiderdown. Where were her bones? Asnah's shoulder blades had grown so sharp, they were like two knives rubbing against one another. "Asnah," Sorrel wept, "what has become of us?"

The dream hung over Sorrel unpleasantly. There was no succor in sleep. Besides, Asnah had not been able to get out of Poland, and the paper said things were very bad there. Letters to her might as well be dropped off a bridge as into a mailbox. Sorrel moved slowly from the couch. Her limbs were as heavy as the lids of cisterns; her heart raced.

She put her hand to her chest, and a throb of fear made her jitter. People said if you ate too much rich food, *schmaltz* would gather around your heart and make it hard to catch your breath. Suppose that was all it was. Ah, but she knew better. She was fattening herself for the slaughter, cramming food down her throat until the monstrous liver would weigh more than a child, and still there would be no birthing.

Yet, who could blame her if she did like a decent piece of bread and a little sweet butter once in a while. There were days when she felt so hungry she could start at one end of the loaf and work her way to the other. She had done it as a girl, she and Asnah together, sitting at a table with bread still warm from the ovens and blackberry jam spooned into a saucer.

Such plans they had made: the handsome husbands, talented children, fine houses. The dreams swirled like tea leaves stirred in their glasses, only to settle as dreams do . . . at the bottom. So her life seemed to her now: the hot sweet gulped down, the dreams a muddy residue.

In the kitchen she sat at the wooden table and ate a lump of cold oatmeal from Tova's dish. The girl ate nothing. Everything in America was diet, diet. So much food and everyone afraid to eat it. She prayed Tova wouldn't turn crazy like Chaikeh's Molly, afraid to take a mouthful of bread and then swallowing Ex-Lax in the bathroom when she got too hungry to stop herself from eating.

Under Sorrel's slippers, spilled sugar crackled on the brown and gray linoleum. Marta was late as usual. Say something and she would sulk and flounce around all day and do less than ever. Sorrel would have to ask her to wash the floor again. The thought of Marta, tight-lipped, sloshing water over the linoleum and leaving it dirtier than before made Sorrel's head ache. Still, who was she to complain when she hadn't the energy or desire to do the work herself?

Sorrel stared down at the floor and watched a trail of red ants feast on the sugar. Maybe she was losing her senses. Why did she feel that everyone was blaming her for being sick? Even in dreams they blamed her. She dreamed one night that she came upon her mother searching the corner of Sorrel's kitchen with a candle guttering in a cracked saucer.

"Look," her mother had scolded, "everywhere in this kitchen they are crawling, the cockroaches."

It was no lie. Sorrel could see them even in the candle's dying light that leapt and danced like an ecstatic Hasid. She felt she could hear them, too, the millions of tiny jaws crunching away at crumbs she had neglected. There on the dream table was a giant roach, shiny brown, its feelers arched ahead, trembling as it savored a flake of cheese her cloth had skipped.

"Sorrel," said her mother, "why do you always leave your dirt for somebody else to clean?"

Well the crumbs could wait; everything could wait. Only she had no time. My God, how she would have wanted to watch Tova grow. Sorrel wiped her nose and eyes with the hem of her nightgown. As for Joseph, let his *nafke* take care of him. They thought because she was sick her senses had left her, but she had seen trouble the day the slut walked into the store with her brassy finger-wave and rouged lips.

Joseph had fallen over himself in his eagerness to

hire her, the easy excuses sliding around in his mouth like *latkes* in a pan of oil. "My wife needs to stay home and rest," he said with the girl standing right there, one hand on her out-thrust hip. And he had hired her on the spot. When Sorrel had whispered in Yiddish, "Come into the storeroom a minute; I want to talk to you," he had pretended not to hear, though Sorrel pointed out later that the girl didn't even know how to keep books. Some office manager!

Sorrel went into the dining room where the tall, black telephone stood in an arched niche in the wall, receiver perched on its shoulder. I won't call, she thought, even as she lifted the receiver and set it down carefully on the shelf. Then, grasping the mouthpiece around the neck, she dialed slowly, quailing at the scrape of the instrument against her fingernails. After one ring, the voice answered, crackled in Sorrel's ear, questioned, and questioned again. Sorrel heard a sharp click. Quietly she replaced the receiver on its hook. Rosie had answered on the first ring. That meant she was in the tiny office and he was probably in there with her.

There was a time, Sorrel remembered, when Joseph would creep up behind her as she stood washing dishes, would press himself against her, cup her breasts in his two hands. "Stop it, silly," she would say, flushed from the steaming water, her hair curling in tendrils about her face—conscious of the color in her cheeks, the nipples hardening under his fingers, he growing stiff

164

against her, both of them laughing. "Stop it! Tova, she'll see." Did he stand that way behind Rosie now as she had reached for the phone?

The unexpected ring caught her like a wasp sting; Sorrel jumped, but did not reach for the phone. Instead she let it ring several more times, standing, hand on her pounding heart. They were clever, but they would not get her quite so easily. After another ring, she picked up the receiver and leaned toward the mouthpiece. "No, I didn't call. I was just cleaning up the kitchen a little. Marta didn't come. Yes, I'm fine."

Was it possible she really was fine? She wanted to believe it, but she only knew that when she asked, people looked at the floor, or up at the ceiling, or out the window. Better not to ask. After the operation, they sat like roosting chickens in her hospital room, her mother and father, her sisters and brothers, aunts, uncles, cousins, Joseph, all of them brooding in low voices, then moving two by two out into the hall from which they returned with cheerful faces as false as Purim masks.

All around her the voices clucked and chattered. Only inside her the stillness bellowed like the echo in an empty well that sent her questions back to her unanswered. The very name of her illness was so poisonous it must be kept secret, for fear that bringing it into the open would contaminate them all. Perhaps they were right to try to fool her. In any case, she only caused them sadness when she asked. They told her to be quiet, to "behave herself" as if she were a child . . . to "calm herself" as if she could.

In her bedroom, the vanity with its triple mirrors gave back many Sorrels. Ranged in front of her lay a celluloid dresser set, shell pink and studded with little green glass stones, a wedding present. She fingered the pieces, one by one, and arranged them neatly: a comb, a hand mirror, a covered powder box, a nail file, a pair of manicure scissors, a buffer, a buttonhook. Almost without thinking, she moved a brown glass medicine bottle, out of place among the dainty grooming implements, into a drawer.

Sorrel loved the idea of things belonging together: a set of china, a set of silver, a tea service, a set of bed linens. She fretted when pieces were missing, stormed around the house for days until the misplaced item was found and the set complete again. There was a symmetry she recognized in nature—in the wondrous twinning of butterfly wings, the balance of bisected fruit. She wanted that prescribed order in her own life.

Untying the wadded kimono, Sorrel allowed it to slip to the floor. She stared straight ahead so as not to see where the thin straps of the night dress rested on her shoulders. The right breast filled the silken cup snugly; the other side of the bodice ballooned like a bellows, in and out. She let the silk ribbons drop from her shoulders, and the gown, too, fell to the rug.

What had sustained her in the past was the notion that nothing was really ever lost, but only set loose in the world someplace waiting for her to be clever, patient, or trusting enough to rediscover it. That was all when she had been a child, of course, before she understood that "lost" did not simply mean that which had not yet been found.

For once she allowed herself an unflinching look at what had been done to her. She was sickened by the lack of symmetry in her body, for while one breast hung like a ripe pear, where the other breast had been, satin scar tissue stretched—still angrily red—and the incision, forking to a jagged line under her arm, looked as if large basting stitches had been poked through a child's sewing card. Was it a wonder that she had to pretend to faint to gain his attention? Who would want to touch such an unbalanced thing? "I'm lost," Sorrel said, softly. "I'm lost."

Sorrel kept her eyes averted from the bed with its blankets still tucked tightly in at the edges as though two monks had shared it. She remembered other mornings when she would primly straighten the twisted bedclothes before Marta came. Now she dressed as quickly as she could, fastening the eyelets of the corset and pulling the laces tight as she tied them. She hooked the corset cover in front of her, twisted it around to the back, and slipped her arms into the shoulder straps. As she sat on the vanity bench to pull on her stockings, she could see the left side of her bodice gaping open and shut like the mouth of a fish. She stood and hooked the stockings, front and back to the garters on the corset, smoothing the silk around her thighs.

From a small drawer, she pulled a piece of pink rubber molded to the form of a breast and slipped it into a pocket in the corset cover. As she raised her arms to draw her dress over her head, the taut flesh under the left armpit refused to give; she clenched her teeth and settled the rayon shift around her hips, pulling the hem straight. Then she lowered herself slowly back down onto the vanity bench. She anticipated the pain this time, and deliberately reached for the comb with her right hand. The rubber breast shifted in its pocket, and once more she had the sense of being askew. Where her strength came from she didn't know, but she forced her feet into street shoes and snatching up her pocketbook she walked out the front door, leaving it unlocked in case Marta ever decided to come to work.

The street seemed to come alive as Sorrel stepped out, almost as if her presence set in motion a world that had stopped everywhere but in the house where she had been grappling with her adversaries. Two boys in caps and knickers rode past her on bicycles, two little girls played on the sidewalk, expertly bouncing a tiny red ball and scooping up multicolored jacks. From far off, she could hear a raucous horn and the cry, "Old rags, old rags!" A scissor's grinder pushed his portable repair shop along the curb in front of her, bell clanging.

Sorrel walked slowly; the spring air rested silkily on

her shoulders, and a bright sun penetrated her bones. Dandelions were suddenly everywhere. Some had advanced to seed pod; some had already lost their heads. The melting islands of snow along with the shovels that stood in every doorway the last time she had left the house were gone.

Time was passing, and there were things she needed to tell Tova. The girl would be a woman soon. For certain she ought not to sit now the way she did with her dress hiked up and her legs apart, but Sorrel couldn't say anything to the child without a pout or a frown for reply. Only yesterday she had suggested that Tova clean her fingernails, and the girl had snapped, "Shut up! You're always after me." When Sorrel cried, Joseph had told her she took everything too seriously. It was only a saying: "shut up." Tova meant nothing by it. Things were different in America. The child was under strain, and so on.

How could Sorrel explain that she wasn't really angry, that she wept because she felt sorrow for Tova. Someday, in some unlikely place—on a slow moving train, or at a celebration, standing in line for something she didn't want, or lying sleepless on an August bed—her daughter would recall the words, Sorrel knew, and there would be no instrument sharp enough to cut them out of her head.

Nearing downtown, Sorrel stopped to rest on a bench in a small park planted with tulips in gaily colored beds of red and yellow. Next to her a gray-haired woman sat with her hands clasped around a large, brown handbag. For a while they both watched a young woman boost a little child onto the nose of a cannon that stood at the center of the park, a memorial to dead soldiers.

"Nice day," Sorrel volunteered, trying to form the English words carefully.

"The days are the same to me since my son passed," the woman answered, as if she had been waiting for an invitation to speak. "I can't stand the house so I come here and sit."

Sorrel looked at the woman and then down at her fingernails. What did it mean, 'passed'?

"Died July ninth, last year," the woman continued in a monotone. "Right after his birthday. I got him a pair of Florsheim's; he always liked good shoes." She wiped her glasses with a red cloth from her spectacle case. "Never could afford to buy 'em for himself after the kids came." She replaced the glasses on the bridge of her nose, gingerly, because of the two red marks glaring there. "The hospital gave back the shoes afterward . . . in a brown paper bag. You couldn't throw them out," she said, defiantly, "There was hardly any wear on 'em."

Hand over her mouth, Sorrel moved her head from side to side in sympathy. That was the way life was, everyone with her own bundle of trouble.

"I'll never be able to look at a pair of shoes in a brown paper bag again," the woman was saying.

Sorrel had thought to talk about her sickness. It was easier sometimes to open your heart to strangers than to those who were too close, but she was ashamaed to speak now. To outlive a child was God's worst punishment. She would have taken the woman's hand, had she been able to remember what comfort meant.

Fifteen minutes later, Sorrel stood on Michigan Avenue across from their store, jostled by people intent on Easter shopping. Now that she was there, she hadn't the nerve to go in. What would be her excuse? He would know she came because she had no trust in him. She imagined them together, he and the girl. Where did they go? Perhaps after the store closed, they would dim the lights and far at the back, away from the show windows that would have presented them as if in a play, they would pull down a flowered carpet from the racks and unroll it on the wooden floor . . .

Sorrel closed her eyes. She couldn't get out of her head the picture of Joseph with his mouth at the woman's breast. Sorrel opened her eyes again. Perhaps she *had* gone off the mark, *meshugge* like Dora their neighbor in Detroit who sat, poor thing, day and night chain smoking Luckies and banging on the baby grand. She shivered at the memory of Dora—blood-red beret on her black bob and spit curls, eyebrows shaved and then penciled into perpetual question marks—squinting from the cigarette smoke and klopping away at the same tune, while her unfortunate mother emptied the ashtrays and wrung her hands. Who knew what voices in her head Dora was drowning out with her music?

Through glass doors propped open to the tender spring day, Sorrel saw rows of orderly counters piled high with shoes and overalls, pencils, crayons, and notebooks. At the gleaming candy counter, a salesgirl, Emma, lifted the scale's scoop and poured multicolored gum drops into a white paper bag. Shyly, Sorrel walked inside, past a rack of house dresses, feeling out of place as though the store belonged to strangers, as though she had not, herself, spent hundreds of hours in the evening arranging folded socks, mating scattered shoes that she had so carefully matched the night before. How many yards of cotton, denim, and oil cloth had she unrolled, measured and ripped from the heavy bolts? How many barrels of dishes had she lifted from excelsior, dusted, and stacked?

Still Sorrel stood, barely inside, in a sense unwilling to commit herself to actually being there. Nearby, a young woman, belly jutting out like a sheer cliff, fingered baby sacques. A boy in a sawtoothed beanie decorated with bottle caps slouched against a counter, reading Big-Little books when he should have been in school. Sorrel could not see Joseph, nor was the bookkeeper in sight.

"Mrs. Mandell! What are *you* doing here? How do you feel?"

Sorrel pulled her shoulders back and tried to walk casually down the center aisle. It was only Josephine who had been with them for years. Sorrel managed a sheepish smile. "I ain't dead yet, Jo," she said.

"Oh, Mrs. Mandell!" Jospehine's cheeks looked dusted with flour under the two coin dots of rouge. "You wait here," she said, too quickly. "Sit down by the shoes, Mrs. Mandell; I'll tell your hus . . ."

"No, no," Sorrel interrupted. "Take care of the customers. I'll find him."

Josephine, a glittering pincushion on an elastic around her wrist, bit the edge of a thumbnail.

"It's okay," said Sorrel. "I know my way."

The office, barely larger than a closet, was empty. So they are together, Sorrel thought, noticing that the door to the basement stood open. So they are down there together. She hesitated at the top of the wooden stairs, afraid she might grow faint and stumble. She wasn't sure she was ready to know what was going on between the two of them. Suppose they *were* checking stock just as Joseph had told her they might do. Then that meant she could trust him to be telling the truth about other things as well. It's very simple, Sorrel said to herself. If they are taking inventory, it's a positive sign. If he has been telling me the truth about that woman, then I am not going to die.

On the street, an automobile backfired with the sound of a gun going off. Sorrel jumped and grabbed her heart, almost fell forward, caught herself. And if he lied? If she found what she believed she would find, what was the advantage in certainty? Speculation, terrible as it was, was the only nourishment left to her. She had better hang on to whatever crumbs remained.

Turning, she walked back down the aisle, past pots,

pans, tea kettles, strainers on one side, and dolls, tops, jump ropes, and toy dishes on the other. Josephine was ringing up ten cents on the register. "Did you find . . ."

"Everything is okay. I found what I needed." Sorrel tucked her pocketbook under her arm. "Take care of yourself, Jo." Then, without knowing why, she added, "Don't take no wooden nickels!"

Sorrel strolled past a few more stores, staring at their windows, seeing nothing beyond her wavering reflection. Stripped of purpose, she wandered idly and found herself, finally, looking at movie stills on the mica-flecked placard outside the Bon Ton Theater. Tova ate lunch in school and would not be home for hours. If Marta was there, the house would be a regular Castle Garden with buckets of dirty water standing and newspapers spread on the damp floor. Her sullen presence filled the house, palpable as the smell of stale sweat that hung in the air after she collected her money and went off, leftover food wrapped in her soiled uniform. If Sorrel couldn't go back to the store, she had also, this morning, given up her claim to her house.

Next door to the Bon Ton, "The Nut House"—only a few feet wide—sat tucked between two buildings. Sorrel felt for her change purse and entered the store. The sweet burnt sugar scent of caramel corn and the roasting nuts bobbing in bubbling oil filled her mouth with water. She had hardly eaten today.

She bought a box of the caramel corn, half a pound of cashews so greasy they turned the white paper bag translucent, a package of Walnettos, and a scoop of malted milk balls.

At the ticket window of the Bon Ton, Sorrel juggled the bags of candy, while she fished for more change. She bought her ticket and entered the smoky lobby, then the theater itself, where she shuffled blindly down the aisle, clutching purse and candy, unable to see anything but the shaft of light from the projector and the black-and-white bodies embracing on screen. Tiny fan-shaped lights attached to the aisle seats cast a yellow glow on the thin carpet under her feet.

Fred Astaire in top hat and tails leaned toward Ginger Rogers in a frilly dress that clung to her bare shoulders. The theater stank of tobacco smoke and the sharp bite of urine. Joseph was right. He had said bums peed in the balcony, although she had not believed it when he told her. She was crazy to have come here alone. This was not a family theater.

The seats around her slowly came into focus as her eyes accustomed themselves to the dark. In front of her the theater was empty; only one man in her row, several seats away. She felt warm, wet under the armpits, and the rubber breast had worked itself up to where she could see it at the opening of her collar. She reached up and shoved it down, then plunked into the prickly, plush seat. In moments the dread washed over her again. The sweets wouldn't help, nor the movie, nor the excitement of the foolhardy adventure that made the pulses in her head pound. She was going to die, and no one would tell her how soon. Sorrel chewed the sticky caramel corn, swallowing it down with a wave of nausea.

It was not easy to concentrate on the movie. Joseph would have called home again, found her not there. Surely Josephine would have mentioned her aborted visit. Had he left the store to check on her, remembering the terrible morning? Or had he already given her up? When he lay with the bookkeeper, did they talk about her, count her years? Perhaps deep down, for she was a woman after all, might she not feel a kinship with Sorrel? But she was young and whole. What did she know from trouble?

Sorrel unwrapped a Walnetto and sucked it until it was pliable. She was aware that the man in her row had changed his seat, moved a bit closer. She should get up and find another seat, or better yet, stop the foolishness and go home. She sat, and he moved into the seat next to her.

A few people were scattered around the theater, but no one else had come to sit nearby. On the screen, Fred and Ginger danced in fluid symmetry, her steps echoing his. Ginger twirled on Fred's arm, her perfect breasts outlined in heavy satin that shimmered like the inside of a seashell. Women didn't lose breasts in Hollywood.

Sorrel felt the fabric of the man's jacket against her

bare arm where it lay on the armrest of her seat. She snatched her arm away as if it had been touched by a live wire. He watched the movie, and she inched her arm back on the chair. When he pushed his leg against hers, she did not move.

She reached into one of the sacks and poppped a malted milk ball into her mouth. A year from now, six months, less perhaps—who knew—her flesh might be dissolved like the sweet. First the one breast, and then . . .? Was it possible to hack off the other? Could humans be butchered like that? At what point did the body say enough?

Sorrel felt the man's hand tentatively touch her calf. Slowly he began to work his way up her leg under the slippery fabric of her dress, sliding along the sheer stockings. She stared at the flickering screen. When he reached the little pillow of flesh between her stocking and her corset, she put out her hand to stop him. Still she said nothing. She could smell tobacco on him and shaving lotion or soap, she wasn't sure which, a spice scent, and it wasn't unpleasant. When he put his arm around her, she did not move but sat stiffly, clutching her purse and the sacks of nuts and candy.

Hand in hand, as the movie ended, Fred and Ginger disappeared in thick clouds of mist. Sliding his fingers down Sorrel's right shoulder, the man began slowly to caress her breast. She opened her purse and groped for the wadded handkerchief. Happily ever after was for movies and young girls sipping tea and jam. When the newsreel came on, Sorrel put her hand in his. Together they watched the hulking tanks snake into Poland. She leaned her head on his shoulder. Eyes straight ahead, they sat, side by side, until the show was over.

WHOEVER FINDS THIS:
I LOVE YOU

was set in Electra by NK Graphics, Keene, New Hampshire. Designed originally as a linotype face by William Addison Dwiggins for the Mergenthaler Linotype Company and first made available in 1935, Electra is impossible to classify as either "modern" or "old-style." Not based on any historical model or reflecting any particular period or style, it is notable for its clean and elegant lines, its lack of contrast between thick and thin elements that characterize most modern faces, and its freedom from all idiosyncracies that catch the eye and interfere with reading.

The book was printed and bound by Maple-Vail Book Manufacturing Group, Binghamton, New York.

Designed by Anne Chalmers.